Didi

Nirupama Devi was part of a new breed of women writers who were winning the hearts of readers in the late nineteenth-century Bengal. Her most productive years as a writer were between 1913 and 1927. Her major novels and novellas include *Annapurnar Mandir* (1913), *Aleya* (1917), *Shyamali* (1919) and *Bidhilipi* (1919). *Didi,* her longest and most critically acclaimed novel, was originally published in 1915. *Shyamali,* depicting the life of a deaf and dumb girl, was adapted into a play and created a stir. Nirupama Devi passed away on 7 January 1951.

A published short story writer and poet since the age of 18, **Alo Shome** has been engaged in translating Bengali classics into English for the last 15 years. Her work as a translator has been praised highly by critics and readers alike. She has translated Bankim Chandra Chattopadhyay's *Krishna Charitra* (published by Pustak Mahal in 2008), Mir Mosharraf Hossain's *Bishad Sindhu* (published by Niyogi Books in 2018), and a collection of Bankim Chandra Chattopadhyay's essays on Hinduism titled *Many Threads of Hinduism* (published by HarperCollins in 2015). *Didi* is Alo's fourth undertaking as a translator.

Didi

NIRUPAMA DEVI
Translated by **ALO SHOME**

RUPA

Published by
Rupa Publications India Pvt. Ltd 2023
7/16, Ansari Road, Daryaganj
New Delhi 110002

Sales centres:
Prayagraj Bengaluru Chennai
Hyderabad Jaipur Kathmandu
Kolkata Mumbai

Edition copyright © Rupa Publications India Pvt. Ltd 2023
Translation copyright © Alo Shome 2023

This is a work of fiction. Names, characters, places and incidents are either the product of the author's imagination or are used fictitiously and any resemblance to any actual person, living or dead, events or locales is entirely coincidental.

All rights reserved.
No part of this publication may be reproduced, transmitted, or stored in a retrieval system, in any form or by any means, electronic, mechanical, photocopying, recording or otherwise, without the prior permission of the publisher.

P-ISBN: 978-93-5702-483-9
E-ISBN: 978-93-5702-458-7

First impression 2023

10 9 8 7 6 5 4 3 2 1

Printed in India

This book is sold subject to the condition that it shall not, by way of trade or otherwise, be lent, resold, hired out, or otherwise circulated, without the publisher's prior consent, in any form of binding or cover other than that in which it is published.

A Short Biography of Nirupama Devi

Nirupama Devi was born on 7 May 1883 at Berhampore in the Murshidabad district of undivided Bengal. She was among the six children of Nafar Chandra Bhatta and his third wife, Yogomaya. If anecdotes are to be believed, Nirupama seems to have been Nafar Chandra's favourite child.

At the age of 10, Nirupama was married to Nabagopal Bhatta of Saharbari in the Nodia district. She lost her husband to tuberculosis just after four years of their life together. She stayed with her widowed mother-in-law until the latter's death a few years later, though the older lady often sent her to be with her parents in Bhagalpur.

Though Nafar Chandra was a highly educated and intelligent man, he was an orthodox Hindu. He was against widow remarriage, believed in the purdah system, and preferred that the women of his household should not come out before male visitors. Nevertheless, he welcomed his widowed child with open arms to his house and made her live there like an honoured and important member of his family. He was often found discussing family problems with her.

Yogomaya—a sensible, down-to-earth lady—encouraged her widowed daughter to forget the past and open her mind to new ideas and happenings. Brother Bibhuti Bhushan, who was only two years older, shared a keen interest in literature with her. Her other siblings, including her half-brothers, showered her with affection.

Even before her marriage Nirupama was fortunate to have friends who loved to write. Indira and Anurupa, granddaughters of Bhudev Mukhopadhya, the renowned nationalist and educator, lived in her neighbourhood when Nafar Chandra was a judicial officer in Chuchura. Anurupa and Nirupama, almost of the same age, called themselves 'Gangajal Soi'. Soi-making is a folk tradition in Bengal whereby two girls become intimate friends after exchanging auspicious items like turmeric, curd and sweets. The friends call each other by the same name—a new name they both agree upon. The tradition is out of practice now except among some small rural communities. In Tagore's novel *Chokher Bali*, 'Chokher Bali' is the chosen name by which friends Ashalata and Binodini call each other and through all ups and downs remain the best of friends and advisers to each other. By a stroke of luck, when Nafar Chandra was transferred to Bhagalpur, Indira and Anurupa's father was working in that city and had his family with him. So, the three girls, all destined to become competent novelists in the future, had a teary reunion when Nirupama came to Bhagalpur as a widow of fourteen.

Indira, Anurupa and Nirupama were part of a new breed of women writers who were winning the hearts of readers in the late nineteenth-century Bengal. The trend started with Swarna Kumari Devi, Rabindranath Tagore's elder sister, who wrote *Deepnirvan,* a historical novel. Published in 1876, it is considered to be the first Bengali novel by a woman. Not only did she write with dexterity herself, but she also took great pains to encourage other promising young girls to write.

Nirupama got a major boost as a writer when her work was noticed by Sarat Chandra Chatterjee. Owing to his father's poverty, Sarat Chandra spent his years as a student in Bhagalpur under the care of his maternal uncles. When the Bhatta family came to Bhagalpur, Sarat was a college student. It did not take long for the older Bhatta boys to get acquainted with Sarat. In fact, it was through Indu Bhushan, Nirupama's *mejda*,[1] that Sarat got to have a look at her notebook of creative writing.

Sarat was, at that time, the mentor for a group of young boys with literary aspirations. Nirupama's *chhorda*,[2] Bibhuti Bhushan, still a schoolboy, become part of that group and because of his passion for writing and his generous nature, developed a close friendship with his 'Sarat Dada'. In *Chhaya*, the hand-written magazine produced by their literary club, Bibhuti submitted Nirupama's writings along with his own. Without meeting the great author personally, Nirupama received his opinion on her prose and poetry through her brother. Later, when Nirupama was an eminent writer and Sarat a more famous one, he continued to comment on the younger writer's works and spoke well of them to critics and publishers.

When Nirupama first came into contact with Sarat Chandra, she must have been 14 or 15 and Sarat in his early 20s. Even though they were not permitted by the orthodox Bhatta family to mix and talk freely, and even though Sarat left Bhagalpur after two years of college in

---

[1] In Bengali, 'mejda' means second elder brother, that is, an elder brother who is the second son of the family.
[2] In Bengali, 'chhorda' means the youngest among all the elder brothers.

search of a job, scandalmongers accused the two writers, who had great respect for each other, of being romantically attached. Several journalists, over many years, have tried to gain cheap popularity by speculating on the status of their relationship. They also forgot that Sarat Chandra was a happily married man for the last 30 of his 62 years of life.

Though Nirupama Devi is primarily recognized as a novelist, her early work consisted of poetry and short prose pieces. Nevertheless, she wrote a long prose work, *Uchchrinkhal,* quite early in life to please Anurupa and Indira, who encouraged her to write more. That work was published 18 years later and is now counted as her first novel.

Nirupama really bloomed as a novelist in her mid-20s and after. Nafar Chandra died in 1907, within a few months of his retirement from office, even before he could relocate to the large house he had built in Berhampore to live in after government service. Now, the rest of the Bhatta family moved there. Here, Nirupama took charge of things, along with her brothers, in the role of an active, responsible and involved householder, occasionally, perhaps, as Durga Das Bhatta reveals, irritating her sisters-in-law by her excessive authoritativeness. Bhatta also records how most of Nirupama's writings were done in the kitchen and pantry area of the house, in between housework. I was struck by what she had written in her diary about house cleaning: 'Must write a few letters now [...] though I am completely exhausted after removing all those cobwebs.

The hands and even my legs are aching.'³ It was amusing to see that the author has used the Bengali word 'theng' to mean her legs. In Bengali, both 'theng' and 'pa' mean 'leg', but 'theng' is never used respectfully. It is reserved only for insignificant creatures. It appears to me that the writer's choice of the term for her own legs in her diary reflects how humble she was at heart.

Nirupama Devi's most productive years as a writer were between 1913 and 1927. The list below notes the years of publications of her major novels and novellas:

Annapurnar Mandir (1913)
Didi (1915)
Aleya (1917)
Bidhilipi (1919)
Shyamali (1919)
Bondhu (1921)
Amar Dairy (1927)
Yugantorer Kotha (1940)
Anukarsha (1941)

Didi is her longest and most critically acclaimed novel.
In 1953, the novel *Shyamali*, depicting the life of a deaf and dumb girl, was adapted into a play and created a stir. In 1956, *Shyamali* was made into a successful film. Later some of her other works, too, were adapted for the stage and the silver screen.

---

³Bhatta, Durgadas, 'Bhoomika' *Rachanaboli, Pratham Khanda, Nirupama Devi,* Karuna Prakashani, Kolkata, 2004, p. 26. (Published in Bengali. Quote translated by Alo Shome.

In 1904, aged 22, Nirupama Devi won the prestigious Kuntalini prize for excellence in story writing. In 1936, the literary convention of the city of Bardhaman felicitated her for her writing talent. She received the Bhubanmohini Gold Medal in 1938 and Jagattarini Gold Medal in 1943 from the University of Calcutta in recognition of her contribution to literature.

Nirupama Devi's years between 1927 and 1940 were devoted more to active social work than to writing. Joining the Civil Disobedience Movement of Mahatma Gandhi, she proudly carried the national flag and marched with other women participants. With friend Sushma Sinha, she took to the streets and went from house to house collecting donations for a school for girls in Berhampore. Their efforts bore fruit when the Maharani Kashiswari Girls Pry school was started in the city. Becoming a member of the Congress Party, she attended meetings in Town Hall, Calcutta, where she spoke in support of widow remarriage. Her activities prove that though she led a restrictive widow's life to please a loving father, she was a progressive person at heart and in her mind.

Nirupama had formally entered the Vaishnava sect of Hinduism quite early in life—when she was still living in Bhagalpur—but became an earnest follower of Vaishnavism only in 1940 after she was introduced to Vaishnava Guru Gour Govinda Bhagavat Swami.

As we know, Vaishnavism is based on an aesthetic philosophy which celebrates the desire of human beings for excellence through Krishna and Radha's sublime attraction for each other. Krishna stands for the Supreme Soul and Radha represents the imperfect but beautiful world. No wonder then that the artistically endowed Nirupama, when turning to religion, would choose *this* particular branch of it.

The last 10 years of the author's life were spent in Vrindavan, a centre of pilgrimage for the Vaishnavas, where she and her mother stayed in a house put at their disposal by her brother-in-law Gobinda Chandra Chakravarty. She remained a meticulous caregiver to her mother until the older lady's death in 1949. Within two years, on 7 January 1951, the novelist, herself, passed away in that holy city.

Translator's Introduction

Nirupama Devi's *Didi* is the story of a diligent, assertive and capable woman who, according to her own admission, loves to be in charge of things. She can take responsibilities and deliver on them as creditably as the chief executive officer of a large company. Yet, in the novel she is only a co-wife with a younger woman who is deeply in love with her husband. As divorce is not an option (*Didi* was published in 1915, years before divorce was legalized in our country by the Hindu Marriage Act of 1955), Surama's challenge is to lead a fulfilled life within the parameters of her weird circumstances.

To complicate matters, Surama continues to love her husband through all the ups and downs in their lives, though she tries hard to hate him. And, from time to time, there is that niggling reminder in her mind that she is a wife still, duty-bound to her husband till death do them part. This terrible, stressful conflict defines and prompts all her actions in the novel.

In that sense, *Didi* is a unique love story which delves deep into the psyche of a wronged wife who not only has a great sense of the right but is also a very warm person. The renowned critic Dr Shrikumar Bandyapadhyay (1892–1970) highly praises Nirupama Devi's Surama. He writes, 'The main character of Nirupama Devi's novel, *Didi*, is a finely drawn, meticulously developed personality. Every gesture of her pulsates with life. [...] The tiniest manifestations of her persona become as clear as daylight to the readers. Compared to this character, even Bankim Chandra and Rabindranath's heroines seem like newly acquainted people or creatures of a poetic imagination.'[1]

There is no villain in the story. Even Amar, who brings home a second wife, is gentle and benevolent. The novelist, very convincingly, makes him a victim of circumstances. The second wife, Charu, a child-woman when the story begins, is extremely fond of her didi, Surama, Amar's first wife. Indeed, Nirupama names her novel 'Didi' as the friendship of the two wives of one man forms the fulcrum of her narrative.

The novel has strong subplots, too, one of which depicts the painful process by which a young widow sublimates her sexuality and submits herself to God, the only way of living allowed to her by the society of her time.

Unexpectedly, though, the plot of *Didi* ends with the protagonist's admission that a woman's place—any woman's place—is always beneath a man. At once, the readers begin to suspect that the only reason for the novelist to give such a sorry turn to her luminous principal character was to conform to the social demands of her time.

In her brilliantly researched paper, Aparna Bandyopadhyay writes, 'The writing of social fiction in the Bengali Hindu colonial context was a difficult and complex process and the anxiety to adhere to the demand of gender ideologies of the

---

[1] Bhatta, Durgadas, 'Bhoomika' *Rachanaboli, Pratham Khanda, Nirupama Devi*, Karuna Prakashani, Kolkata, 2004, p.18. (Published in Bengali. Quote translated by Alo Shome.)

time was at times in conflict with a spirit of interrogation and defiance. [...] Reading these novels leaves an impression of an uneasy ambivalence, of creativity plagued by dilemmas and contrary pulls.'[2]

And yet, to my mind, the beauty—including its structural poise—of Nirupama Devi's novel has not really been compromised by the restrictions alluded to by Ms Bandyopadhyay. In fact, the absolute defeat of Surama's ego at the end of *Didi* could have been a preferred choice by the author to emphatically point out how society needed to change for women to live their lives with dignity.

---

[2]Bandyopadhyay, Aparna, 'The Politics of Reading: A Study of the Critical Responses to Nirupama Devi's Novels' *They Dared: Essays in Honour of Pritilata Waddedar*, Simonti Sen (ed.), Gangchil, Kolkata, 2011.

PART I

Chapter 1

It was a winter afternoon. The bare branches of frost-damaged trees were soaking up the warmth of a blissfully sunny and cloudless day, somewhat rare for the season.

There was a wood next to the village through which a narrow path—lit by sunlight filtered through the criss-crossing leaves and branches of trees—coursed, looking like a smile on a frail face. A spotted dove called plaintively from within a bamboo bush. On a high branch of a lemon tree, a pair of wild pigeons debated with each other, voicing their opinions with alternating high and low pitches that echoed throughout the woodland. Bees buzzed around a drumstick tree whose branches, shaken by gusts of breeze, dropped white flowers and yellowed leaves on the wayside. On the ground, flocks of gleefully chattering robins, starlings, babblers, bulbuls, treepies and other birds were enjoying their afternoon break.

The village beyond was quiet. In the middle of the tiny compound of a small hut, the householder's pet dog had fallen asleep in the comfort of sunny warmth. Even the parrot in its wicker cage hanging from the roof of the hut had stretched its wings to sunbathe.

Two young hunters, guns on their shoulders and killed birds held tightly in their grip, emerged from the woods and took the village path. One said, 'Deven, are you still angry with me?' The other replied, 'Yes because I am really disappointed at not being able to shoot more than just this one ruddy shelduck from the whole flock.'

'But, what of that! Haven't we bagged enough of partridges and quails?'

'Cannot compare them with a large shelduck. And, it is all your fault, Amar. What's the point of being kind to game birds when you have come prepared to kill them?'

Amar smiled guiltily but did not go on to defend himself as something else had caught his attention. Deven followed his friend's gaze. In front of the cottage they were passing by, a girl aged ten or eleven, with long curls adorning her face, was squatting and playfully shifting the dust under a mango tree. When an elderly widow came to gently rebuke her, the child looked up and smiled. The two friends, Deven and Amar, were close enough to perceive the beauty of that smile and the charm of that blue-eyed girl's innocent face. The kid was like a blooming rose in a humble garden.

Deven remarked, 'Found something pleasant to watch?'

'Yeah. And haven't you?'

'Oh, I know them very well. The girl is Charu. She is like a kid sister to me. Now, hurry up. I want to go home and have some tea.'

'That's right, we need some tea. My limbs are aching after the exertion.'

In a while, the two friends reached a two-storeyed house—Deven's residence. Hurrying in and putting down his load of game, Deven lit a stove and set a pot of water on it to boil for tea. Amar stretched his legs on the bed. Before long, he said, 'I was thinking of leaving this place tomorrow. Don't want to offend my father by taking too long a break from studies.'

'Stay for two more days,' pleaded Deven. 'Remember, we won't be seeing each other often from now on—only when you make an effort to come here, or I make time to visit you. Surely, I won't be going again to Calcutta anytime soon.'

Then the friends had their tea and got busy with other things.

The next evening, Amar found Deven dashing into the house with a tense expression. Picking up his medical kit, he was about to leave again when Amar asked, 'Where are you off to?'

'To a patient,' said Deven. 'Her mother had called me. And who but a destitute person would call a doctor who has yet to get his certificate? I have just visited her. The patient is in a bad condition. Has an odd kind of fever, probably remittent? Has a very high temperature.' Then Deven remembered, 'You know the girl! She is Charu. Why don't you join me in treating her? It will be a great help to me. Do come.'

Amar could not refuse. Indeed, he was not at all unwilling to accompany Deven.

The patient, her face flushed, lay on a low, unkempt bed, her mother caressing her brow.

The two friends examined Charu thoroughly. Then, after instructing the mother about her medication and care, they returned home.

Amar was to leave for Calcutta the next day, but Deven was reluctant to let him go, saying he needed his assistance in treating Charu. So, Amar could not return to Calcutta as scheduled.

After a tireless vigil and apt treatment by the two friends, the fever left Charu on the eighth day. Her widowed mother blessed the two medical students again and again. Now, there was also time for the mother to enquire about Amar's whereabouts. She was especially pleased to learn that Amar was her *swagotra*.[1] 'Charu, do *pronam* to him. He is a respected elder to you,' she instructed. Charu raised her head from the pillow and gestured her obeisance. Amar, smiling, twirled her hair.

In a few days, Amar returned to Calcutta and his medical studies. He attended lectures in the college as well as made speeches as a representative of his institute. In his free time, he enjoyed theatre shows. Memories of his visit to Deven's village and those of Charu's illness were fading fast from his mind.

Babu Haranath—the zamindar of Manikgunj and Amar's father—was the owner of a large house, a huge motor car and a big belly. Though a strict man in general, he had a soft corner for his only child who had lost his mother. Keeping him happy and fulfilling all his wants was one of his passions. He was a kindly person otherwise too, and treated his subjects well. His charitable habits were well known and held responsible for his not attaining great wealth as a zamindar. Even his bitter rivals—the family of the Basus—had to admit that Haranath's *zamindari*[2] was not thriving as much as it should only because of his unselfish nature.

The Durga Puja season had come. One day when Amar

---

[1] This indicates that Amar belonged to the community into which the widow's children could marry.

[2] Zamindari was a system of land ownership and taxation that was prevalent in India during the Mughal and British colonial eras. Since the zamindari system was marked by inequities and exploitation, it was abolished in India in 1951.

was getting ready to leave for his home in Manikgunj, Devendra visited him in his dwelling in Calcutta. He invited Amar to accompany him to his village to spend the puja days there. Devendra had just qualified as a doctor and, as thanksgiving to Ma Durga, his mother was observing a special puja. Deven tried to persuade a reluctant Amar. Should not Amar join in the celebrations as a close friend? Were not the two of them like brothers?

Amar was moved. Having lost his own mother in childhood, he had a weakness for the idea of motherhood. If he could, in some way, contribute to fulfilling a mother's wish, he was ready to do that. So, along with the shopping required for the ceremony, which was the main reason for Deven's visit to Calcutta, he took Amar to his village.

Ritualistically, Deven's mother's Durga Puja was not as flawless as pujas in Calcutta were, but Amar was impressed by the simple joy and devotion with which the villagers participated in the celebrations.

On the tenth day, after the immersion of the idol, it was time for people to exchange auspicious greetings. Hugging his friend, Deven said, 'Do I really have to bid adieu to you today?'

'Yes, Deven. Even though my father readily agreed to my spending the puja days with you when I wrote to him about it, I know how eagerly he must be waiting for me.'

'And I suspect, you, too, are very keen to see him. Looks like you are still a little boy.'

As the friends were talking, a group of small girls approached them to pay their respects. Taking turns, they touched Amar's and Deven's feet. Among them, a girl in an indigo sari was especially attractive. Noticing that her looks pleased Amar, Deven asked, 'Can you recognize her?' After thinking for a few moments, Amar recognized her. 'Isn't she the kid we had treated once?'

Deven nodded and proceeded to greet each of the girls individually. 'Go inside my house, girls. My mom is waiting to treat you with sweets.' The pretty girl in blue approached Deven and said softly, 'My mother requests you to come to our place once, Deven Dada...'

'Of course, we will go there. Did not need an invitation for that,' replied Deven. 'Come, Amar, let us go and pay our respects to Charu's mother.'

'But will there be enough time?' Amar wondered. 'Remember, I have to catch a train this evening.'

'I know, I know. I promise I'm not going to delay you for that. Will only make a flying visit to Charu's mother.'

In her little cottage, the poor widow had arranged a meal for Deven and Amar by setting two plates with the best of sweetmeats and savouries that she could manage to procure. She was overjoyed to meet the two friends. Amar was, frankly, overwhelmed to find her so excited on seeing him. 'I can never repay your debts,' said the widow.

'Aren't you an aunt of mine? Isn't it our duty to look after you?' Deven cheered her.

'By the way...' the widow had something more to say but the friends had no time to listen to her as they had to leave, at once, for the railway station.

∞

As the two friends walked side by side, Deven softly said, 'The widow has no one to look after her and her child. Just because I speak to them kindly, she feels she can rely on me—as if I am somehow related to her. But you know my difficulties, my family problems. You also know my financial challenges. I have got to work very hard to support my family. No scope for me to do anything worthwhile for the widow and her daughter, however much I may want to.'

'Is she *that* poor?' asked Amar.

'No. What she worries about is not money to live on. She wants her daughter to be married well.'

'But isn't the daughter just a kid?'

'She is eleven. How much longer than that can a Hindu girl remain safely unmarried? The widow has started looking for a groom in earnest. She fears that if Charu is not married off soon, she won't get a good husband due to the meagreness of her dowry. Now, Amar, do me a favour. Help me find a groom for her.'

'Such a good-looking girl,' said Amar, reflectively. 'She is bound to get a good husband even without a dowry.'

'Don't you have any idea about the world around you, Amar?' said Deven in surprise. 'Do you think that a well-qualified boy or a boy from a rich family will readily marry her? Only money speaks in this world. I agree that she is a remarkable girl—not only for her beauty but also for her charming nature. But she lacks that vital element—a good dowry to accompany her.'

'I don't believe that the world is so mean,' said Amar, slightly agitated.

'Oh yes, it is,' snapped Deven, 'especially the affluent part of it. A suitable boy from a poor family may be found occasionally to marry without a dowry. But that magnanimity will forever be missing from the moneyed class...'

'That's not true,' objected Amar, 'greed may exist in

some families but...'

'Don't give me examples from what is written in modern novels. Come down to earth. Show me which rich boy has married without a dowry. Let us take *you* as an example, for the time being. I am sure that proposals for your marriage are already coming to your dad from rich, illustrious families. Won't you willingly marry one of their girls?'

'You are being unfair to me by assuming things. And if I marry into a wealthy family, it would only be to respect my father's wishes and the wishes of my other elders and not because I myself want to marry for money.'

'It means the same thing. Their wishes will make it more convenient for you to find a wealthy bride.'

'Now, please stop criticizing me using hypothetical situations. You're making it sound like I am already a culprit.'

'I am sorry,' said Deven. 'I can speak my mind only with you. But, do forgive me for my outburst.'

The friends had reached the bullock cart that would take Amar to the railway station.

Seated on the cart, Amar bent down to look at Deven and said, 'You have asked me to try to find a groom for Charu. I will surely be on the lookout but...'

The wheels of the cart had started rolling noisily, rendering the ending of Amar's sentence inaudible for Deven. But Deven smiled to himself, thinking that he had already found a groom for poor Charu.

Chapter 2

Having spent a few days in the comfort of his own home and being lavished with goodies by his father, Amar heard from Diwan Shyamacharan that his marriage had been fixed. The would-be bride, Surama Devi, was the daughter of Radhakishore, the zamindar of Kaligunj. A beautiful girl, she was about thirteen or fourteen years old. Amar's father, Haranath Babu, had gone himself to meet the girl and had returned completely satisfied after finalizing the match. 'A very sensible and good-natured girl,' the avuncular diwan added. Shyamacharan was his father's assistant and the manager of his estate.

Amar wanted to ask, 'How sensible? Will she be able to look after our lands?', but held back from being sarcastic towards the diwan. Amar was not happy on hearing about this unexpected development. However, it was difficult for him to express his disapproval of a match so enthusiastically fixed by his father. The excuse 'Why so soon?' seemed too flimsy. The excuse 'I do not want to marry a rich girl' also sounded hollow as he had never before mentioned any such criteria. His father would be surprised to suddenly hear such a statement from his son, and some of his relatives would, perhaps, prescribe special oils to cool his head. Moreover, it was not as though his father had rejected any poor family in favour of a rich one. It was not for her riches alone that he had selected Surama, his future daughter-in-law. Somehow or the other, Amar could not say 'no' to the match.

As soon as the few days left of the month of *Kartik* had passed and *Agrahayan* had begun, Surama and Amar were married.³ Considering that the bride was a beloved daughter of Radhakishore among his three children and that Amar was Haranath Babu's only child, the wedding was celebrated on a lavish scale. Everybody said it was a good match. Even the Basu family admitted that Zamindar Haranath had struck a good bargain with his son's marriage.

Amar, however, could not invite Deven or even inform him about this important event. There was no reason for Amar to care about Deven's opinion on a desirable match. Deciding whether to accept Surama or not was entirely a private matter for Amar and his family. Yet, he felt a pang of guilt at not living up to Deven's expectations. He was, therefore, not in a hurry to let Deven know what he had done. Amar realized that the news of the wedding would spread, and Deven would, surely, hear about it sooner or later.

Fulsajja, the first night the bride and groom spend together in a flower-bedecked bed, was not very romantic for Amar and Surama. Amar felt awkward in the company of a girl he had met only during the wedding rituals.

As was customary, the bride left for her father's house after a few days, leaving little scope for the couple to get well-acquainted before the separation. Amar took leave of

---

³'Kartik' and 'Agrahayan' are the seventh and eighth months of the Bengali calendar. This calendar was conceived by Emperor Akbar and prepared by a team of Persian and Indian scholars. It is a solar calendar aimed at matching the time of tax collection with the harvesting season.

his father and returned to Calcutta. When he received a letter from Deven requesting him to visit his village again, Amar did not reply.

When it was Durga Puja again, Amar visited Manikgunj. Surama was expected to join him there, but unfortunately, her mother had expired suddenly. She wanted to stay with her father for a few more months. Haranath, although disappointed, did not hesitate to allow Surama to stay back with her father.

Amar thought of writing a letter of condolence to Surama but abandoned the idea. A written note to a person he knew so little would be too formal for his liking. It would be better if he expressed his genuine feelings when they were together again.

Eighteen months passed after Surama and Amar's wedding without them really being together. Another holiday had come and Amar was about to leave for home when a letter, again from Deven, arrived at his Calcutta residence. Deven had written, 'Please come over. If you don't, you will regret it for the rest of your life.'

Amarnath could not ignore that strange request.

Smiling, Devendra welcomed Amar when he reached his house in the village. 'What is the matter, Deven? Why did you call me?' asked a worried Amar.

'Nothing is wrong,' replied Devendra. 'You have stopped visiting me. So, I played a little prank.'

'No, Deven, you should not have done this. We are not children anymore...'

'What is the harm? You do not have a wife at home to ask you where you are.'

Amar blushed at this remark but could not say anything.

In the evening, Deven asked, 'Amar, you remember Charu?'

'What about her?' enquired Amar, adding 'Is she dead?' as a light joke, though at the same time, Charu's innocent smiles and her pallor during illness came to his mind.

'No, she is alive, but her mother is dying. I am treating her. Come with me. I will be going there to check on her now.'

'I hope the girl is married,' said Amar.

'No, not yet. She belongs to a community where boys do not marry without a dowry—that is, she belongs to your community.' Then, after a moment's pause, Deven added, 'But *you* had promised to look for a groom for her. Didn't you? I am sure you have somebody in mind. We will be glad to accept your choice.'

Amarnath vaguely remembered agreeing to look for a groom for Charu but had no idea that it amounted to a full-fledged promise. He had not taken the matter seriously enough and had taken no action on it. However, Deven's expectations, somehow, made him feel guilty.

They reached the small cottage which Amar had visited a few times during his earlier sojourns in this village.

The patient, thin and pale, lay on a narrow bed with her eyes closed. Charu, grim and worried, sat beside her. The girl blushed on seeing Amar, who thought, 'How silly of her!'

After a few minutes, when the dying lady opened her eyes, Deven announced, raising his voice so that she could hear clearly, 'Aunty, Amar has come!' 'Where?' she asked excitedly. Deven pushed Amar close to her.

Amar was amazed to see the joy and excitement on her sickly face. 'Charu,' she called faintly. When the girl approached, the mother, trembling, took one of her daughter's hands and joined it to one of Amar's, saying, 'I give my Charulata to you. May God keep you happy.'

Amar was so stunned that he lost his voice for a few moments. When he could speak, he shouted into the patient's ear, 'You cannot do this! Don't you know that I...'

Deven intervened, pulling Amar away. He said, 'I know you have things to explain to her. But, do it later. As a doctor, I request you to let her sleep for a while.'

Amar waited, but soon Charu's mother grew worse; her breathing was getting heavier and heavier. Realizing that he needed to act immediately, Amar pushed away the sobbing Charu and yelled into the mother's ear, 'I cannot take Charu. I am already married. Didn't you know that? I am a married man!'

But the mother was unconscious—her physical powers, including her sense of hearing, were already with the Almighty.

Deven was astonished. 'You are already married, Amar? Without even letting me know?'

Amar replied, 'You are probably not pretending. Maybe you really haven't heard about my marriage. That is possible because I did not write to you about it. But, what have you done! You made that poor lady believe that her daughter is married to me. I wanted to tell her the truth when she was conscious, but you forced me not to...'

'I am not at fault, Amar. God is my witness. I did what I did without knowing that you were married. I thought the explanation you wanted to give her was that your father won't approve of your marrying Charu.'

The patient died at dawn. Deven called a group of boys from the neighbourhood and took the body for cremation.

Amar did not know what to say to the bereaved Charu, who wept bitterly as she rolled on the floor. So, he just sat, deep in thought. Even a few hours ago, the girl would not have known how helpless and alone she would find herself in this world. Was she very disappointed that Amar could not marry her?

A few days passed. Amar had to leave for Calcutta soon. 'What do we do with Charu?' he asked Devendra.

'Don't know,' replied Deven.

'Keep her with you and look for a groom. I will pay for her dowry,' said Amar.

'Charu is not of our caste,' said Deven. 'My mother will never allow her to live with us. And I cannot trust you to pay for her dowry. You will forget all about it as soon as you leave this place. The best thing would be for you to take her along. Find a good guy and get her married.'

Terribly irritated and angry with Deven, especially because he had hurt his ego by calling him untrustworthy, Amar was in no mood to plead further with his friend. Finding no other option, he decided to take Charu to Calcutta. He considered it a fit punishment for his own mistakes, including his failure to inform Devendra about his marriage with Surama.

Chapter 3

Initially, Amarnath toyed with the idea of finding a place for Charu in the abode of one of his friends in Calcutta, but, on second thoughts, he realized that this might create problems of its own. People might begin to spread rumours about the two of them. Moreover, after Deven's refusal to welcome Charu into his family, Amar felt sure that others would do the same. A Hindu girl of marriageable age was a huge liability for her guardians.

With no alternatives available, Amar reluctantly took Charu to his own quarters in the city, hoping that nobody would be too curious about her. His college break was spent helping the girl to settle down. He cancelled a scheduled trip to his village after giving his father some lame excuses.

Amar had a large accommodation in Calcutta. So, fixing a room for Charu was not a problem, nor was it difficult to find an elderly maidservant to look after her. With kind words spoken tenderly, Amar was able to help Charu reconcile with her new situation.

When the college reopened, Amar went to his classes regularly. He also began to look around for a boy who would marry Charu. He did not tell his father what he was going through, not having the heart to reveal Charu's pathetic condition to anybody—not even his own father. Marriage with a suitable boy would change her status. Amar would, then, have no qualms about telling her story to anybody. It would hardly matter, he reflected further, even if the issue was never disclosed to the zamindar. After all, Charu was only a short, passing phase of his life.

And yet, the vision of Charu's mother on her deathbed often disturbed him. He was unable to ignore that she died believing her daughter was safe with him. He did not know how to come to terms with the memory of that incident. Deciding that the best way out was to get Charu a good match, he intensified his search for a groom. During this time, he received a letter from Deven, who wanted to know whether Charu was being looked after well. Amar, angry and irritated, did not reply to it.

Monsoon had arrived and dramatically altered the appearance of the city. Even with doors and windows closed, residential buildings were battered by the rains. Pearly raindrops came down on rooftops from an overcast sky. The *kadamba* and *shirish* trees, next to a particular house, were full of blossoms. Flowers, whose names Charu did not know, growing on potted plants arranged in rows on the terrace, sent their faint fragrance through an open window. As Charu watched the downpour through the window, tiny droplets sprayed by the rain glistened on the loose ringlets of her hair.

Charu remembered her village. There, she would climb to their attic to watch the rain. Along with the sound of raindrops, she would hear frogs croak and crickets stridulate. And she would smell the exquisite scent of wildflowers. She recalled how the claps of thunder would scare her mother, who called out to her: 'Oh, Charu, come down! You are getting wet. Come down to me...'

Suddenly, a voice interrupted her thoughts, 'Charu, you are getting wet...' It was Amarnath, who had just entered the room. Charu moved away from the window.

Noticing tears in her eyes, Amar asked, 'Why are you crying, Charu?'

Receiving no answer, Amar enquired again, 'Don't you like the room I have furnished for you?'

Charu hurriedly replied, 'I like it very much.'

'Then, what is making you cry?'

'I miss my mother. Mamma asked me to be near her whenever it rained hard.'

Amarnath came to the window and closed it. He pulled a chair and took his seat. Pointing to another, he asked Charu to sit as well. A diffident Charu obeyed.

'Charulata, you still remember your mother and cry for her. I know how dear she was to you, and how much she loved you. But she is no more. Doesn't anybody else care for you, Charu?'

With a voice choking with tears, Charu replied, 'Nobody, except you!'

Amar smiled and asked, 'Did you think up the phrase "except you" just now? Didn't you remember it when you were standing at the window shedding tears?'

Charu blushed as she lifted her face, shy but pleased, and faintly uttered 'no'.

Smiling again, Amar asked, '"No" in what sense, Charu? In the sense that the phrase did not occur to you suddenly or in the sense that you did not remember me then?'

With some cheer in her voice, Charu said, 'I always remember that you care for me, that you love me. Mamma used to say so.'

Amar was stunned. He was not prepared for such candid words from Charu.

'Innocent girl,' he thought, 'does not know how to speak tactfully.' He decided not to take her seriously. Instinctively moving his chair a little away from her, he was silent for a while. Charu, too, remained quiet with her eyes cast down. A few minutes passed. Then, clearing his throat, Amar began, 'Yes, Charulata, that is the reason why I am taking time in choosing a suitable groom for you. I want to hand you over only to a deserving man. But we won't have to wait much longer now. An excellent proposal for your marriage has come to me at last. I feel you will have no reason to object to it. My duty towards you will be fulfilled on seeing you happily married.'

Charu sat as still as a statue. After a pause, Amar continued, 'Don't feel shy, Charu, to think about your marriage. You are a big girl now. As I don't know any relative of yours, I have no option but to speak to you directly about this matter. Charu, I sincerely believe that the boy I have found for you will make you happy.'

Though Amarnath was trying to make his position as clear to Charu as possible, he hardly expected an answer from her. From his earlier attempts to draw Charu out, he had learnt that she became absolutely silent whenever the subject of a groom for her came up. Amar felt that this reticence stemmed from something more than just her childlike innocence. He was curious to uncover what lay behind her attitude.

'Okay, Charu, are you ready for this marriage?'

Charu kept as quiet and still as before.

Her reaction, or the lack of it, conveyed to Amar a

vague possibility of something he was afraid of.

He needed to make Charu understand her exact position in the world, and for that purpose, he needed to know her mind first. To begin with, Charu had to express herself more freely, Amar reflected. He knew that Charu enjoyed speaking about her fondness for animals and people. So, to get her talking, he asked, 'Tell me, Charu, who were the people in your village whom you loved dearly?'

Lifting her face, Charu began to slowly enumerate, 'Mamma, Bhulo the dog, my pet parrot, Deven Dada, his sister Suku, you...'

'Me!' exclaimed Amar. 'I am not an inhabitant of your village, surely!'

'But you had come there a few times. And you had cured my illness. Mamma loved you so much. She used to remember you often. Deven Dada used to give me your news and relate stories to me about your family.'

Amar was aghast. Cursing his friend Deven in his mind and pretending to be casual, he said, 'Okay, Charu. When you are married to a man as good as, or even better than, me, do love him as much.'

'No,' said Charu.

Amar shivered. 'Why not, Charu?'

'Because you love me.'

Amar did not know what to make of that. But he carried on as casually as was possible for him, 'Yes, Charulata, he will be very fond of you, I guarantee. He is a rich man with a large house and many servants. I think there will be playmates for you, too. Aren't you happy to hear all this? The boy is also very good-looking. He plans to take you home as soon as the two of you are married...'

Amar had to stop as Charu began to sob, covering her face in her hands and lowering her head on the armrest of her chair. Amar touched her head gently and, as if scolding her, said, 'What is this, Charu?'

'I don't want to go,' moaned Charu. 'It will kill me!'

Amar stood up and was unable to move. The vague awareness that he had wanted to suppress was now undeniably clear in his mind. The tear-stained and pained child-woman was so plainly declaring her love for him—confessing that she did not want to be anybody else's.

He was truly at a loss for words. But, was he unhappy? No. How could he be? How could he not cherish something which even gods might wish for? A simple village maiden's first bloom of love, offered to him with all the sincerity of her heart, was not something he could trample on. He had not loved anyone intensely enough, nor been loved deeply enough, to feel spiritually bound to a previous relationship. His past had no emotional connection strong enough to hold him back from accepting what Charu had to offer. It was true that he wanted to do his duty to Surama. He knew how enraged his father would be if he neglected that duty. Those were the reasons why he had got so deeply involved in looking for a suitable boy for Charu. As a matter of fact, one could not swear that he sometimes did not feel sad at the prospect of giving Charu away to another. She had always charmed him. And in the proximity that was forced upon them now, the exquisite expressions of her clear, blue eyes had often disturbed him.

That would not have prevented him, though, from doing right by Surama. But now there was a major roadblock. Although he hadn't intended for it to happen, every cell in his body was filled with joy. Charu was his! Charu loved him. Knowing this, how could he not respond by loving her in return?

Amar sensed that Charu had always loved him, perhaps, because her mother had given her the impression that she belonged to him. He realized that all the while he was hunting for a groom, she considered herself betrothed to him.

The vision of Charu's dying mother making him promise that he would accept her daughter as his wife came to him again. He remembered that his objections had not reached the dying woman's ears. Amar's stunned looks had probably made her believe that he had accepted her daughter. The memory of that episode filled Amar with renewed energy as he believed that it represented a real promise he had made to her.

He instantly made up his mind: he would marry Charu. Polygamy was accepted by his religion even if modern society did not approve of it. He did not care much for society's views. What mattered to him, though, were the responses of his wife and his father. Perhaps they would forgive him when they learnt about his dilemma. It was not as though he was driven by lust. He would have to marry Charu to fulfil his moral obligations.

Gently lifting Charu's face with both his hands, he called her in a tender voice, 'Charu!'

Charu looked at him. Her eyes were brimming with tears.

'Do you really love me so much?'

Charu nodded to indicate that, yes, she did.

'You can't think of leaving me and going away?'

Charu nodded to say that was true.

'Then, are you ready to marry me, Charu?' asked Amar.

Charu nodded her assent.

'Do you know, Charu, that I am a married man? That I already have a wife?'

'Yes, I know,' said Charu. 'I heard you telling that to Deven Dada.'

'And you are still ready to marry me?'

'Yes,' said Charu, innocently, 'because you love me.' And she began to sob again.

'Though I love you, Charu, I sincerely believe that you would be happier with another man. That is the reason I have searched for a good match for you. If you marry me and don't get along with my first wife—if she hates you, for example—your life would be full of troubles and that would hurt me too. Better to be with somebody who will have only you as his wife. You can remain in his company like the Goddess Laxmi of his household.'

Charu, again, lowered her head on the armrest of her chair. She covered her face with her hands and uttered between sobs, 'I will die if I go there.'

'But you know that I already have a wife, and if you marry me, you might have to face great difficulty. Do you still want to be my second wife?'

Charu nodded to say 'yes'.

Then, holding up Charu's face as gently as if it were a lotus flower and looking deep into her eyes, Amar urged, 'Then, Charu, promise me that you will always love me as much as you do now in spite of the challenges that lie ahead of you and the stigma attached to being a second wife.'

Still sobbing, Charu replied, 'I promise.'

Chapter 4

Amarnath was resting on a couch in an elegantly furnished room, which was made fragrant by the *shefali* flowers that bloomed outside the windows. It was evening and the time for Durga Puja was once again approaching. The melodious sound of *shehnai*[4] issued from a nearby temple, along with invocations to Goddess Durga.

Amarnath had come home to his village a few hours ago, leaving Charulata behind in Calcutta. This was an important visit as he had come over to convey to both his wife and father his intention of marrying Charu. He hoped that they would understand the gravity of a promise made to a dying woman.

Feeling that his wife's goodwill was more important to him than that of his father, he had decided to speak to Surama first.

The cosiness of the room and the comfort of his couch had made Amar drowsy. He was half asleep when the door opened gently and Surama entered. Finding Amar on the couch, she came directly there.

Though a carpet was spread on the floor, the faint sound

---

[4]The 'shehnai' is a musical instrument that is commonly used in Indian classical music and played during weddings and other important festive occasions.

of her footsteps broke Amar's stupor and he exclaimed, 'Who is it?'

Surama had grown during the months Amar had not seen her, and he could not recognize her. In any case, he had met her only in festive settings. When the visitor announced that she was Surama, Amar looked at her in wonder. Once a slip of a girl—shy and bejewelled—she had turned into an elegant lady, looking at him with dark, intelligent eyes.

Amar could not bring himself to speak. Surama waited for a while, staying where she was. Then she moved about the room, arranging knick-knacks, before turning towards the door to leave.

'Listen, please!' Amar called her before she left.

Surama came and stood before him once again.

'Sit down, please,' requested Amar.

Not finding a chair nearby, Surama sat down on the couch, a little away from Amar. Finding him silent, still, she reminded him, 'You called me?'

'Yes,' said Amar, but lapsed into silence once more. He seemed to be rehearsing the speech in his mind.

'Do you have something important to tell me?' asked Surama, sensing his discomfort. 'Is it about me? Have I offended you in some way?'

'No, no,' said Amar, hurriedly. 'But, yes, I have something to tell you. It is about a pledge of mine. You must listen to me carefully as it has far-reaching consequences for us.'

'Please begin,' said Surama, 'I am listening.'

Slowly, Amarnath related the whole matter to Surama, omitting only his recent intimate exchanges with Charu. He recounted how he met her for the first time in Deven's village and how he had assisted Deven in treating her when she was ill. Amar described in detail the interactions he had with Charu's mother. Amar even related the conversation he had with Deven about Charu before he left for the railway station on Dussehra evening.

It was after that trip that Amar's wedding to Surama had taken place. He explained to Surama that Deven, Charu's mother and Charu had come under the impression that he would like to take Charu as his wife. This was something he wasn't aware of.

Amar ended his narrative by describing the scene of the elderly widow dying with the conviction that he would marry her daughter.

There was a long pause when the speech was over. Then Surama asked, 'Where is the girl now?'

'The girl? Charu? She is in my bungalow in Calcutta.'

'I see. So, she must be living there for the past four or five months. I wonder why you did not tell us about her before!'

Amar was irked. He said, 'I don't think it matters. I don't think I have committed a crime by not telling you about her earlier. I am telling you now. It is the same thing, I am sure.'

'Perhaps, not exactly the same,' said Surama, gently. 'You could have brought her here to live with us.'

Amar was rather vexed now. 'What is the difference?' he retorted. 'Both the houses belong to us, don't they?'

'There is a difference, nevertheless,' said Surama. 'Here, she would have been in the company of your father and your wife.'

'There is no harm in living with the girl I am going to marry later,' responded Amar.

'It cannot be as harmless as you think,' insisted Surama. 'But I don't want to argue with you on that. Now, tell me, have you really made up your mind to marry her?'

'Yes, of course! What else can I do in this case?'

Surama paused to reflect, before answering, 'Perhaps *now* you have got no alternative, but surely, there was a time when she could have been given away to some other suitable boy.'

'What is the difference between now and then?' asked Amar, boldly.

Surama's bright eyes flashed as they met Amar's. 'Because *now* you have fallen in love with her. Earlier, you hadn't.'

Amar stood up in anger. 'Very selfish of you to say that. Suppose I love her now. What difference does that make? My obligation to marry her is as valid now as it was then.'

'Fine,' said Surama. 'Have you come here to seek my permission? Do you consider that your duty as well?'

'Of course not! However, I thought it was my obligation to inform you.'

'Good. Have you informed your father?'

'You need not worry about that.'

'What if the message upsets him?'

'I can't help it. I have to keep my promise at all costs.'

'So, you are adamant?'

'Absolutely!'

Surama paused to take a deep breath, then said, 'If you don't have anything more to tell me, I will take my leave.'

'As you wish.'

Surama stood up, lingered for a while, and then left the room.

Chapter 5

The next day as the zamindar had his lunch, Surama sat close by with a palm-leaf fan in her hand.

Babu Haranath ate absent-mindedly, worry writ large on his face. 'Dear Child,' he gently addressed his daughter-in-law while having his meal.[5] 'Do you know that Amar was home? Did he meet you? Has he told you anything?'

Surama nodded. She told her father-in-law that they had met and that Amar had informed her about his decision to take a second wife.

'Then you know everything,' the patriarch said with a sigh. After a short pause, he suddenly raised his voice, 'The scoundrel! Doesn't he have any sense? Like an idiot, the chap wants to chop his own head to keep a vow! Who does he think he is—a modern-day Bhishma?[6] Calcutta has

---

[5] A translator is sometimes called upon to use a word in the target language which is not exactly its synonym in the source language, to make it sound natural. In the novel, Zamindar Haranath and his assistant, Shyamacharan, address Surama and Charulata as 'Ma', which means mother. However, it would not sound natural in English if a young girl/woman is called mother by her elders. So, I have used the word 'Child' (in the sense of 'a beloved younger woman') instead of 'Ma'.

[6] Bhishma is a prominent figure in the Mahabharata. He is the son of King Shantanu and the River Goddess Ganga. When his father Shantanu falls in love with and marries a fisherwoman named Satyavati, Bhishma

spoiled him and I am to be blamed for sending him there for his studies. Anyway, I have given him an ultimatum. I will disown him if he does what he wants to do. Yes, I will not set my eyes on him ever again!'

Surama looked down but continued to fan him. Her father-in-law spoke again, gently, this time. Intending to console his daughter-in-law, he said, 'I don't think he would venture to do what he says. I have asked him to return to Calcutta immediately and to come back with the girl. We will settle her down with a good match somewhere.'

'That won't be possible, Father...' said Surama, hesitantly. 'I have to tell this to *you* because I do not have a mother-in-law. And, perhaps, it won't be right to deprive him of his property...'

'Do you think so? Why?'

'I mean, if he cannot honour your wishes, let him do whatever he wants. Why force him to stop?'

'You can say that because you are young,' said Haranath. 'When your child acts like a baby and is about to jump into a turbulent sea, you would want to hold him back with all your might. Even if you need to press him so hard against your chest that it makes him cry, you would not let him jump in.'

Surama was moved by the depth of Haranath's love for his son. Overwhelmed, she whispered, 'Alas! That I would lose such kindness and affection...'

Even before she could complete her sentence, the old

---

takes a vow of lifelong celibacy, relinquishing his right to the throne to ensure that Satyavati's sons inherit the kingdom. The 'terrible' oath earns him the name 'Bhishma'.

man said with conviction, 'Do you think this situation will diminish my affection for *you*? No, my dear. I care for you now even more than I did before. It is only for you that…' He paused for a few seconds as his voice choked, then continued, 'I failed to make you happy in this house, my child. How can I forgive myself?'

'Don't be sorry for me, Father,' replied Surama. 'That makes me feel so selfish.'

'Selfish? Who can have the heart to call you selfish?'

'Even so, it is true that I am the only hurdle in this case.'

The old man tried to say something, but could not find the right words.

'But, Father, you are not eating anything,' said Surama, looking at the zamindar's plate. 'Won't you try the fish? I cooked it. And the dalna curry?'

'Of course, I will,' Haranath answered, taking some fish. 'I like this. Now, about that girl…'

'Just a minute, Father. Let me bring you your milk. It is heating on the stove in the kitchen.'

Surama returned with the milk in a bowl and a smile on her lips, pretending to be amused. 'Father, here is a test for you. Taste this milk and tell me if I have mixed sugar in it.'

Babu Haranath, realizing that his daughter-in-law wanted to end their distressing conversation, acted as if he was cheerfully joining in the game. 'I am sure, girl, that you have put sugar in this,' he said, taking a sip of the milk.

'Wrong!' said Surama, smiling. 'The milk is sweet and thick because it is from our new cow.'

Her father-in-law, who had begun to miss his son by that time, suddenly said, 'Amar has left without eating anything.'

Surama stopped smiling.

'A curse of the planets upon us!' sighed the old man.

⚶

In a few days, it was *Sashti,* the beginning of Durga Puja. The private shrine of the zamindar's residence was full of activity and fun. With the assistance of a group of ladies, most of whom were relatives, Surama was arranging the various items needed for worshipping the goddess. With her own hands, she was efficiently setting the auspicious tray containing offerings that would welcome the Devi. On a nearby podium, decorated with sacred leaves, an invocative symphony in praise of Durga was being played on the shehnai.

Somebody asked, 'Where is Amar? Hasn't he come home for Durga Puja?' The diwan replied, 'His studies have perhaps kept him back this time. A letter from him—addressed to his father—has just arrived.'

At that moment, a maid approached Surama, bearing a message from her father-in-law. He wanted to see her immediately.

Surama met Haranath, who was waiting for her near the staircase beyond the veranda. He had a letter in his hand. 'See what the scoundrel has written,' said the zamindar, who was filled with resentment towards his son.

'What is it, Father?' asked Surama.

'See for yourself.' With hands trembling in agitation, he passed the piece of paper to his daughter-in-law. Surama read:

Respected Father,

I greatly regret that I could not fulfil your wish. It was impossible for me to change my mind. I will be getting married to this other girl, soon.

Your worthless son,
Amar

Looking down, Surama returned the note to the zamindar.

'The rascal! Let him not think that I will ever forgive him,' said the zamindar as he tore the letter to pieces. 'This is the end of my relationship with him—at the beginning of this year's Durga Puja.'

Surama, composing herself, returned to the shrine and continued with her work.

Chapter 6

Before mailing the letter which his father received on the first day of Durga Puja and tore after reading, Amar had returned to Calcutta from his village. He was pained and disturbed, struggling with emotional turmoil.

It must be his father's ego, Amar had reflected. The thought that his son's actions would tarnish his image must have made the old man furious. How powerful can ego be! Any threat to it can change a person's temperament instantly.

Amarnath had met Charu's elderly maid while he was going upstairs. 'Thank God, you have come back! I was so worried,' she exclaimed.

'Why? What happened? How is Charu?'

'She is down with a fever. But I called the doctor. He has given her some medicines.'

'Good. That was wise of you. Hope she is better now. I will go and check.'

He had entered Charu's room noiselessly. She was lying on the bed with her eyes closed and her face flushed. Amar had stood and watched.

The memory of a time two years ago had come back to him. Then, Charu had lain on a shabby bed in a dilapidated cottage, almost senseless with a high fever. She had grown a little since then but looked almost the same. Now, her bed was tidy, her room well-kept, and her clothes decent.

But in a deeper sense, she was wealthier then than she was now. Then, she had possessed the love of a devoted mother. Now, she was a beggar at the mercy of an unrelated, hard-hearted man who could crush her at will. Charu would have lived and died like a wildflower in her own village, unknown to the outside world. But now she had been plucked from there and thrown into a cruel city. Amar had blamed himself for Charu's plight. Everything had happened because he had gone to her hamlet and struck a chord with her and her mother.

Amar had come forward and gently touched Charu's brow to check how hot it was. The contact had woken her. 'You came back? When?' she asked.

'Just now.'

'So soon? But you wanted to spend the puja days there.'

'Yes, I still do. I will go back there tomorrow. And, if you can come with me, I will take you along. My father wants to have you there.'

This had made Charu sit up excitedly. 'I would love to go there!'

'Don't get up, Charu. You still have a fever.'

'The doctor said I'll be well very soon. When are we going home?'

'We can go as early as tomorrow. But why are you so keen to go there?'

'Because it is your home.'

'Yes, it is my home. But that doesn't mean it is a safe place for you. Don't you know how unwanted you are by my family? Don't you know what wrong you and I have done to them?'

'Wrong? What wrong? Will they scold me a lot?'

'I don't think so. Most likely, my people will keep you comfortable...'

'Then, it will be nice to be there.'

'But they will expect you to be apologetic for the way you are related to me.'

'I don't understand. But I won't mind it as long as *you* are there with me.'

'Charulata, you are impossible! No, I can't be with you there.'

Then, suddenly, Amar had started to rave and rant, 'Have mercy on me, girl. Leave me alone! Save me from ruin! Get married to another man! Let my father find a groom for you!' As he said those words, he had taken hold of Charu's face in both his hands and shaken it a little.

The fury had left Amar as suddenly as it had come. He had looked at Charu. Her head was again on the pillow. Her eyes, wide and unblinking, were staring at him.

'What is it, Charu, are you very scared? Don't panic. Go to sleep.'

Obediently, Charu had turned to her side and closed her eyes. Pulling a chair, Amar had seated himself near her bed.

That night, the girl's fever had risen to a hundred and five degrees. Amar had bathed her head with cool water and eau de cologne. Her maid kept on fanning her brow. In her delirium, Charu had moaned, 'Don't take me there. They will kill me.'

That was when Amar wrote that decisive letter to his father. He had felt blissfully relieved. He lay down on Charu's bed—a little away from her—and had a long, peaceful sleep.

Charu's temperature became normal after a fortnight. A few days later, she could sit up on the bed and smile, which convinced Amar that the crisis in her life was over.

Early one morning, the girl woke up to hear that she was going to get married that day.

⁂

After their wedding, Amarnath took Charu to a quiet suburb of Calcutta. He settled down with her in a small, rented cottage with a charming garden. He did this to keep his romance hidden from the prying eyes of society. Amar feared that any unnecessary contact with worldly people with set ideas of right and wrong might jeopardize the exquisite love he felt for his bride. The world, engaged in its mundane affairs, was too insensitive to appreciate the magic of their love. And Amar needed to cherish that love, above all, to soothe the pain he felt at his family's rejection of him.

However, there was hardly any money for them to live on. One day their old maid met Amar and said, 'Master, as you had told me, I got Hari to sell your watch, chain, ring and the other things you had given me. But there is nothing else left with me to sell now and money is running out. How do I run the house?'

'Thanks for your concern,' said Amar, 'I will be taking up a job soon and things will improve. Unfortunately, I could not complete my medical studies. That will make it difficult to find an employer. However, I will be leaving for Calcutta shortly. You must take good care of Charu while I am away.'

Chapter 7

Zamindar Haranath was a disciplined man. The separation from his son did not bring any change in his lifestyle. He woke up early every morning. After washing up, he meditated and prayed for three hours. By eight o'clock, he was in his office, managing his estate.

During luncheon, Surama attended to him. He was determined that she should not feel neglected, in any manner, in his household and tried to involve her not only in matters of housekeeping but also in matters of zamindari. He never forgot to praise her cooking and anything she did to run the house better.

After his afternoon siesta, he spent his evenings in a large study where scholars from various disciplines came to meet him. There were discussions and debates. Good ideas, articulated well, were appreciated and rewarded. The conferences invariably ended with the sounds of pandits, his guests, putting silver coins received by them in their pockets and then saluting the zamindar.

Before dinner, Haranath regularly had a smoke in his private room. This was also his time to talk leisurely with Shyamacharan. And he always asked Surama to be present when the two men were talking so that she would have an idea about the state of their assets.

On one such evening, there was a reference to Amar.

Haranath was reclining on his bed, puffing away at his hubble-bubble. Surama, sitting at a corner of the bedstead, was gently waving her palm-leaf fan. Since the weather was pleasant, she didn't need to wave the fan. But a woman should not sit idle; she must always do something with her hands for social approval.

Shyamacharan was sitting on a chair close to the zamindar's bed. He had returned from Calcutta earlier that evening and was enthusiastically describing a minor victory of the Mitras over their rivals, the Basus. As he concluded his report, he observed, 'Unfortunately, the boundaries of their land and ours are still so badly disputed in so many stretches that we need to be on our guard all the time to protect our rights. I wonder who will take charge of such things when you and I are gone.'

'Why, that is the reason I call Surama to be with us here. Dear Child, try to follow whatever Shyama says.'

Surama nodded.

For a while, nobody spoke. The zamindar took a few quick puffs at his pipe.

'If you permit me, I would like to tell you something...' said Shyamacharan, hesitantly.

'Dear Shyama, why do you ask for my permission? Haven't I given you the right of a younger brother? Tell me freely what you have to say.'

'Yes, I know that you have given me the right of a younger brother. But, as far as rights go—what about birthright?'

'Don't beat about the bush, Shyama. Tell me exactly what you mean by that.'

'I mean, isn't it Amar's birthright to be your heir? Doesn't he have a claim on your property?'

'Don't bring up that subject. What is done is done. Leave it at that. Just tell me who were the people you met in Calcutta. Did you see your own relatives? Are they doing well?'

'Yes, they are fine. Met some other interesting people, too.'

From the manner of his diwan's delivery, Haranath could guess which person he was hinting at. He couldn't control his curiosity. 'Who were the people you met?' he asked.

'I met Radhacharan, Sashikanta, and I met our Amarnath, too.'

Before he could stop himself, the zamindar asked, 'How is he?'

'Just the way you want him to be,' said the diwan, sarcastically.

'Innuendo again! Tell me straight. Is he not keeping well?'

'Health-wise, he is not too bad. Otherwise, he is. He is hunting for a job.'

'Looking for a job? What about his studies?'

'He can't go to college anymore. No money to pay the fees.'

Haranath took a few quick puffs and snapped at Surama, 'Please stop fanning me. I don't need the breeze.'

Surama put the fan down gently and was about to leave the room.

'Don't go!' ordered Haranath.

Surama sat down at the corner of the bed again.

Nobody spoke for a few minutes. Finding his master silent, Shyamacharan continued to make his point. Coughing a little, he began, 'This does not reflect well on you. His material needs will perhaps make him seek your forgiveness—he will just make a show of it—while at heart he may be cursing you. Is that desirable?'

After some reflection, the zamindar asked, 'Did he say that he needed money?'

'No, he didn't. But I invited him to come home with me, saying that even if you did not pardon him, you might extend him some sort of financial assistance. He said he did not have an appetite for that kind of mercy. He added that he will come home only when *you* called him and accepted him just the way he was.'

'Rather gutsy, what?'

'No wonder. Isn't he *your* son?'

'Why did you say, then, that he might come home to seek my forgiveness for want of money?'

'I was speaking of the future. He is bound to come to you when the state of his finances deteriorates further even if he was far from feeling remorseful. As I was saying, all this does not augur well for you. People know he is your son. And he is looking for a petty job. Why let the outside world know you have differences with your son? That you are displeased with him is enough punishment for him. Why withdraw financial support?'

Haranath was listening with rapt attention. He rose from his reclining position. 'You must be tired, Shyama, after your journey,' he said. 'I won't detain you any longer. Go home and rest. And, Surama, my child, it is late for you too. Have your food and go to bed. Don't wait for me. I am not hungry tonight.'

'Won't you have anything at all, Father? Not even some milk?' asked Surama.

'Okay, send me some milk through Rama. And ask him to turn off all the lights.'

When the room was darkened, the zamindar shut his

eyes and waited for a welcome stretch of sleep, but he was too emotionally agitated for slumber. A series of images flashed before his eyes—images of his early youth, his marriage and his love life. He remembered how fervently he wanted a child in those days, and how, after years, his wish was fulfilled. He recalled his joy at becoming the father of a tiny little fair boy! He got goosebumps just remembering how he had felt then.

Our memories have a strong hold on us. We often move on in life, leaving behind a sad or a happy place to start anew amid new friends. But the memories of our earlier neighbourhood can still control our moods. They can make us sad when we are expected to be happy, and happy when we should have been sad.

The zamindar, sleepless, went on thinking about his past. He remembered how tragedy had engulfed his family when his child was only two years old. Amar had lost his mother all of a sudden. How he had clasped the child close to his breast! Haranath tossed and turned in bed as he recalled that moment. Sleep came after many hours, but his dreams remained filled with visions of his single parenthood.

Waking up in the morning, he started his day as usual. At mealtime in the afternoon, he ate in silence. Surama noticed his grave expression but made no comment. Finding him so sombre, Shyamacharan, too, took care not to bother him.

After his evening prayers and a light snack, he called his diwan to his room as usual. As was the norm, Surama was also invited and she took her place at the corner of the large bed, palm-leaf fan in hand.

After some small talk, the zamindar, pretending to be casual, said, without raising his eyes from the newspaper he held in front of him, 'Dear Shyama, thinking over the matter very carefully, I have decided to send him a monthly stipend. And that will be only for the sake of my own prestige.'

'Good!' said the diwan. 'It will be nice if Amar accepts it.'

'He has to!' remarked the zamindar, raising his voice a little. 'He is duty-bound to accept that much for the sake of my honour.' 'Surama,' he called his daughter-in-law, 'shouldn't he be getting some monetary assistance from us? State your opinion clearly.'

'No,' said Surama in a clear, steady voice.

'No? I had not expected that from you! Why shouldn't he get some financial assistance from me?'

'I mean, Father, if you cannot forgive him, why give him anything at all? He is your son. He deserves to be forgiven by you.'

'I agree,' said the diwan, hurriedly. 'What you are doing to him does not suit a kind man like you.'

'It's not so easy to forgive him,' said the zamindar. 'Tell me, Surama, can you forgive him? If you can, I will too.'

'I cannot!' declared Surama in a voice which, though full of emotion, was strong and unshaken. She walked out of the room with firm, steady steps, leaving an echo of her negative statement that hung heavy in the air.

The next day, one hundred rupees were sent to Amar, but they came back within four days along with a note:

Respected Uncle,

I understand that you have pleaded with my father to make this arrangement for my financial benefit. I thank you with all my heart but am unable to accept your kindness.

Though Amar's note was addressed to Shyamacharan, it was the zamindar who sent a reply:

> People know that you are my son. So, some of my prestige depends on what you do. If you take up a petty job, it will smear my reputation. Therefore, until you are well off in life, a sum of one hundred rupees will be sent to you every month, and you are duty-bound to accept it. Except for this, I will not maintain any contact with you.

The message was acknowledged in a few days:

> Even though it feels like torture to accept your money when you do not even call me your son, I will take it to save you from dishonour.

Haranath was relieved, not because his dignity had been at stake, but because Amar would be able to provide for himself and his family.

Chapter 8

Some people can rise from the ashes. Whether by mistake or false pride, they sometimes make choices that seem to ruin their lives forever, but they can also pull themselves together and achieve success in the end. Amar was a prime example of that. Within eighteen months of marrying Charu, he had reorganized his life and worked extremely hard to earn a legitimate medical degree, overcoming one of the greatest challenges he had ever faced. Of course, he still needed to figure out how best to make use of his qualification.

Charu remained as childlike, innocent and dependent as before. Amar was like a swimmer in the sea of life who clasped the inexperienced Charu in one of his arms while navigating the rough waters with the other.

A relative, the son of the sister of Charu's father, had been staying with the newlyweds. He had apparently been a welcome addition to the family. On the one hand, Tarini acted as Charu's housekeeping tutor, and on the other, he kept her company. He, thus, freed up more of Amar's time for studying and attending college. One wonders how Amar would have carried on with his medical studies if Tarini had not been there to take care of Charu. Naturally, Amar was very grateful to Tarini and excused his noticeable character flaws.

One day their elderly housemaid entered their living

room and left a letter on the sofa. Charu picked up the envelope to hand it over to Amar but stopped short on seeing the name on the envelope.

'What is it?' asked Amar.

'I wonder who this letter is for,' said Charu.

'Must be for me or Tarini,' said Amar.

'No, it is for neither of you. It is addressed to me. Now, who needs to write to me?'

Amar also found this strange.

Opening the envelope, they found that the missive was from Manikgunj and was signed by Surama Devi.

'Who is she?' asked Charu.

'Don't you know?' said Amar, quite grave and thoughtful by now. 'Read the letter and you might be able to figure it out.'

Charu concentrated on reading the note. Soon her fingers were trembling and her face was pale.

Amarnath hurried to Charu and took her hand, asking anxiously, 'What is it, Charu? Is my father well?'

'No. It seems he is quite ill. But, maybe, I did not understand the message correctly. Please read the letter yourself.'

Amar took the letter and read it:

Dear Graceful One,

You must be wondering who this letter is from. But once you read my message and convey it to your husband, he would tell you who I am. And both of you will, then, understand why I had to write this note to you.

Our father-in-law is very ill. In fact, he was not

keeping well for the past one year. His condition is quite critical. That is the reason I have written to you on his behalf. He is eagerly waiting to see you both. Please come over immediately. However, do not get too worried as he is feeling a little better today.

Bring with you some good grapes and pomegranates from Calcutta as we rarely get them here.

I have nothing more to tell you for now.

With kind regards,

Surama Devi

After reading the note, Amar was speechless for a while.

'What does she say?' asked Charu.

'My father is very ill.' After a pause, he continued, 'Quick, Charu, pack up some clothes. We have to leave at once for home. Dad is ill.' He called his brother-in-law, who emerged from an inner room. 'Tarini, please help Charu pack her things. We are going home by the night train.'

'Why? And, why all this hurry?' asked Tarini in surprise.

'Received a letter just now, saying that my father is ill.'

'Oh, Master is ill? But does he want you to be there?'

'Of course, he does! Why wouldn't he?' said Amar in irritation.

'Don't shout at me,' said Tarini. 'I just wanted to make sure that the zamindar has written to you himself to say that he has forgiven you.'

'Of course, he has…' began Amar. But he had to pause. Images from the past two years of his life flooded his mind. The suddenness of receiving a letter from Surama and the news of his father's illness had made him feel like a little boy missing his father. Tarini's words, striking him like the stings of a hundred scorpions, jerked him into reality. As things stood then, he did not have the right to run to his dad without checking several facts. Amar moved slowly towards a couch and sat down.

'From whom has the letter come, Amar Babu? The zamindar himself?' Tarini asked again.

'No.'

'Then, who has written it?'

'Whoever it is, is not my dad.'

'It is my elder sister,' put in Charu. 'The letter is written by her.'

'I see,' said Tarani. 'If Amar Babu will take my advice, he should at least not take you there. Let him go alone, if he must.'

'I suppose that will be sensible,' Amar readily agreed. 'You stay back with Tarini, Charu. I must go. Father has asked for me.'

Tarini was quick to comment, 'But the letter is not from your father.'

'My father is ill, Tarini. So, another person had to take down his message.'

'But the zamindar could have asked his diwan or some other official of his estate to write for him. Instead, it is written by your first wife. Don't you understand that it is entirely her doing? She wants to trick you into something.'

Amar's hands flew to his head as he sank into deep thought. 'Yes, you might be right, Tarini,' he said. 'Perhaps, it is not my father who has called me. So, perhaps, I should not go.'

'Let us go, please,' pleaded Charu. 'My didi has asked

us to do that. And, it is surely your father who has called us. That is what Didi has written.'

Amar found himself ignoring some of his own doubts on seeing Charu's absolute faith in what her 'elder sister' had written.

'Tarini, can't it be possible that my first wife's message to us really speaks the truth?'

'I just wished to caution you, that's all,' said Tarani, petulantly.

Chapter 9

Amar was in a state of turmoil when he and Charu took the night train to his village. He did not speak much. Sensing that her husband needed to be left alone, Charu kept quiet.

After disembarking from the train, the couple took a horse carriage to reach their destination. It was early in the morning. Amar's village, just about a mile away, was dimly visible through the surrounding vegetation.

A glimpse of his birthplace reminded Amar of how much he missed his home. It brought tears to his eyes. The wide fields of mustard on either side of the road, the tall trees in the nearby orchards—one belonging to the Basus and the other to the Mitras—looking like spirited contestants, the small bridge over the 'disputed' stream, cowherd boys swinging from a peepul tree—every spot looked mesmerizing to Amar after a long absence. He knew who lived in the thatched cottages. All of them—Hari, Punte, Nyapla and others—were his friends. The memories of his friends came back to him. He remembered the ups and downs of their lives.

As the carriage came to a stop in front of the gate, Amar jumped out of it, his feet pounding over the red cobblestones as he raced to the staircase that led up to the main hall of their house. Somebody standing on top of the stairs called him. 'Dear, Amar, don't be in such a hurry...' It was Shyamacharan Roy. Amar looked up and met his gaze. 'Sorry, I could not send the car to the station for you. Could not guess when you would reach. Master is not well at all...'

'I know, Uncle,' said Amar as he swiftly climbed the stairs.

'Go upstairs. He is in the main bedroom,' directed Shyamacharan.

Then, the efficient Shyama sent an assistant to bring down Amar's luggage from the hired carriage and pay for the ride in case Amar had forgotten to do so in a hurry. The boy who went to get the luggage found Charu sitting in the vehicle. Upon learning that, Shyamacharan ordered the carriage to be brought to the porch of the house. A matronly help was called upon to attend to Charu.

Amar quickly ascended the stairs to the first floor and rushed into a large room bordered by a veranda.

He looked at his father's broad brow, his serene, kind face, his eyes closed in fatigue. He was so overcome with emotion that he began to sway. He made his way to where the zamindar's feet were and lowered himself onto the carpeted floor. Without opening his eyes, the zamindar addressed Surama, who was sitting close by and gently massaging his brow. 'Child, who is it sitting at my feet? Is it Shyamacharan?'

Surama did not answer at once. She was careful not to give the zamindar a shock.

Amar looked up and met Surama's clear and patient gaze, which had no trace of bashfulness in it. Instinctively, he looked down.

The patient spoke again, 'Child, had I fallen asleep?'

'No, Father, you are awake.'

'But I thought that I dreamt of him coming and sitting at my feet. It cannot be true because he is in Calcutta. Has Shyamacharan come to see me?'

Amar could not control himself any longer. Teary-eyed, he put his head on his father's feet.

The zamindar spoke again. 'Child, please check who it is.'

'Father, open your eyes and look for yourself,' said Surama.

'No, Child. I fear that will break my dream.'

Trembling with emotion, Amar called out in a loud voice, 'Father, my father!'

As if struck by lightning, his father's eyes opened. 'Amar!'

The zamindar called Amar again, stretching his right arm towards him. As he sat down next to the bed, Amar took his father's palm and caressed it fondly. The zamindar placed his other hand on his son's head and began to weep like a child. His pillow was drenched in tears.

After a short while, he was somewhat relieved of his sorrow. He looked around for his daughter-in-law, calling out her name.

Surama tactfully stood in a corner, keeping some distance so that the two men could reunite properly. When her father-in-law summoned her, she came and stood by his bed. 'Sorry, Child, I have forgiven him. Could not hold back any longer,' said Haranath.

He continued, 'I will not ask *you* to forgive him, but I have a request to make. For the few more days that I have to live, behave as if you have forgiven him—at least in front of me.' Surama nodded, indicating that she would comply.

'And, if you can, sometime in the future, do forgive him.'

Haranath turned towards his son, 'Have you come alone, Amar?'

'No, Father.'

'You have brought your younger wife, then? But, where is she?'

'In the carriage.'

'As careless of you as ever!' the zamindar chided Amar.

On the orders of Shyamacharan, Charu had already been ushered in. A distant lady relative had been told to attend to her. Charu was waiting with her in the next room.

Soon, Charu was brought in with her head and face covered by the *aanchal*, a loose end of her sari draped over her features. She was trembling with nervous tension as she slowly approached her father-in-law's bed.

Amar sat grimly on a nearby chair. Surama tried to stay aloof by busying herself with mixing the patient's feed.

Welcoming his younger daughter-in-law, Haranath said, 'Come, Child.' As Charu approached, she touched her father-in-law's feet. 'Come this side, Child, and sit on my bed.' With trembling limbs, Charu pulled herself together and came to sit where she was asked.

Requesting Surama to come near, the zamindar took one of Charu's hands and joined it with Surama's right hand. 'Dear Child,' the invalid addressed her, 'please take custody of your younger sister. I put her under your care.' Then, looking at Charu, he said, 'Touch your elder sister's feet. She is no less than a goddess!'

When Charu stood up from bowing and touching Surama's feet, Surama embraced her tenderly. Yes, Surama was looking as dignified as an idol, and Charu thought she could see only kindness in her eyes. Charu lay her head on Surama's breast and softly called, 'Didi!'

Despite Amar's efforts and Surama's sincere and tireless

care, Haranath did not live long enough to enjoy the reunion with his son.

One day when several members of the household were present in the sickroom, Amar had asked the zamindar, 'Father, if you have any special wishes regarding the distribution of our wealth, please tell me. I will carry out your wishes gladly to ensure your complete satisfaction.'

Haranath had whispered weakly, 'Special wishes? No, except that, everything that we have should come to you.'

'But Uncle Shyamacharan says you had spoken to him once about wanting to leave all our property to Surama, your older daughter-in-law.'

'Yes, I had said that to Shyama when I was yet to discover how noble-hearted my older daughter-in-law is. I realized later that such an arrangement would never make her happy. How can I do something that will make her feel guilty all her life? She is as dear to me as my mother was. How can I displease her?'

That same evening, Haranath had breathed his last.

Chapter 10

Amar emerged from his mourning early, for the sake of Charu. After Haranath died, Surama left Amar and Charu to themselves. In that huge mansion, unfamiliar to her, Charu had spent her days sitting alone in a corner, not wanting to disturb even her husband, who was grieving. Wiping away his tears, Amar decided to look after his wife.

Haranath's *shraadh*[7] ceremony was held with great solemnity and respect, with mourners paying their heartfelt tributes. Even his rivals, the Basus, had to admit that Amar had given a fitting farewell to his father. In order to ensure a high standard of the ceremony, Amar had to incur some debts. The zamindar's philanthropy had left little ready money for his son's use. Though Shyamacharan and Surama were not in favour of such extravagance, they refrained from voicing their concern out of respect for a son's sentiments.

After a few weeks, Shyamacharan requested a meeting with Amar to discuss the intricacies of zamindari with him. When he tried to broach the subject, Amar said in surprise,

---

[7]'Shraadh' is a Hindu ritual of paying homage to one's ancestors. It is a way of expressing respect and gratitude to those who have passed away and is a means of seeking their blessings. Shraadh involves offering food, water and other items to the departed soul, along with recitation of mantras and prayers.

'Uncle, why should I bother about such things when you are there to look after us?'

Shyamacharan said that he wished to retire from his job so that he could spend the rest of his life in the holy city of Varanasi. 'Your father, who was like an elder brother to me, has left us. Now I have to be spiritually disposed to leave this world, too.'

'You mean, you want to make me an orphan again, Uncle?' said Amar.

Once again, Shyamacharan tried to convince Amar about his need to retire, but the young zamindar excused himself and left the room.

Finding Amar so uncommunicative, the diwan came to Surama to express his desire to retire. 'No, Uncle, you cannot leave us now,' said Surama, emphatically.

'Why, Child,' urged Shyamacharan. 'I know how reasonable and understanding you are. Then, why stop me?'

'When Father is no more, your absence can ruin the Mitra family forever. Please stay!'

'Child, let Amar handle things now that he is here. You do not know him yet. He is not really a bad boy. And you can help him manage his affairs. Don't stay aloof. Befriend him.'

Surama looked thoughtful. Then, casting her eyes down, she said, 'Uncle, it is not that I am avoiding him without any reason. As the present master of the house, has he asked me for any help?'

She continued, 'Uncle, don't go away, please. We are your children. Don't leave us just when we are making a mess of things. Forgive me for displeasing you, but I cannot yet assume my previous role. I understand how difficult things are right now, but does the current master of the household care about that?'

Shyamacharan fell silent, unable to respond.

A few days later, an irritated Amarnath wanted to see the diwan. 'Uncle, can you tell me why there is no proper housekeeping in this place?' he asked when they met. 'I find that the beds aren't made and the rooms are dusty and not well-lit. Don't we have somebody to keep things in order?'

Shyamacharan briefly responded, 'Maids are there for the upkeep of the rooms.'

Accountant Chandi Ghosh was standing nearby. He said, 'The housemaids have quarrelled amongst themselves. As a result, Bama and Khanta, who cleaned the upper floors, have left. In fact, the maids have created so much chaos in the servants' quarters that our regular cook, Narayan Thakur, has also left. Before leaving, he said that now that nobody supervised the staff, it would be impossible for him to work here any longer. After a desperate search for a replacement, I managed to engage Tiwari as a stand-in last night.'

'Shameful!' exclaimed Amar, looking at Shyamacharan. 'How can such things happen under your supervision?'

'I don't do housekeeping,' said the diwan tersely. 'But, yes, somebody has to do it. You can take charge together with your young bride.'

'But I am not at all interested in instructing servants. Tell me, who was in charge of this department when my father was alive?'

The diwan did not reply, but the accountant said, 'Our mother, the elder mistress of the house, used to look after everything. She was so strict that nobody dared to speak loudly.'

'You mean my older wife? Why isn't she on duty now? My father is no more, but she is not yet dead. Why has she stopped her work?'

The diwan remained silent. The accountant thought for a while, but had no proper answer to give.

Amar asked again, 'Uncle, can you tell me why my older wife has stopped looking after the house?'

Shyamacharan spoke up. 'I suppose that's because you haven't requested her to do so.'

Amar furrowed his brow. 'Not justified,' he said. 'Did I ever tell her what to do and what not to do? So, why should I tell her now?'

'This estate once belonged to your father,' said Shyamacharan. 'It was he who had bestowed upon her the responsibility of running this house. As you are the master now, *you* have to hand over the charge to her.'

'So, are these the drawbacks of being a master? Okay.'

Amar decided to meet Surama the same day. However, when he reached the common veranda that bordered a row of rooms, including Surama's, he stopped. The meeting was not going to be easy, he felt. How would he begin the conversation? What exactly would he tell her? He scolded himself for hesitating. What he was going to demand was well within his rights. So, why should he allow himself to be nervous?

Trying to appear at ease, he entered his older wife's room.

Surama was sitting near a window, stitching something with wool. Hearing footsteps, she turned around and met Amarnath's gaze. Caught unawares, she did not know what to do but quickly regained her poise. Surama put the wool in her workbox and was about to greet her husband with a smile and a 'hello' when Amar spoke up. 'I want to discuss something with you.'

'You want to speak to me about some work that needs to be done?' she asked.

Amarnath was put off by the way she spoke. It reminded him of the day many months ago when he had come to ask her to make a big sacrifice. The memory irritated him. It seemed to Amarnath that Surama expected nothing from him except to make demands that involved labour and misery. What right did she have to make fun of him with hurtful overtones?

He controlled his temper and replied, 'Yes, it is about something that needs to be done. And, it seems, I have to take some of your time to disclose the matter to you.' He pulled a chair closer to where Surama was and sat down.

Surama noticed how hard Amar was trying to act casual. So, she also made an effort to be informal. She smiled a little and said, 'But if you want to finish your talk early, I won't keep you.'

After a minute of silence, Amar began, 'Uncle Shyamacharan regrets that you don't take any interest in housekeeping these days.'

'Did Uncle complain about that to you? I can't believe he did.'

Feeling embarrassed, Amar replied, 'No, it wasn't exactly a complaint from him. In fact, it was I who complained about the shabby state of our rooms. I was told that you used to take care of the management of the household. I was wondering why you have stopped doing that now?'

'You wonder!' exclaimed Surama.

'Why? What's so strange about that?'

'Of course, there is something strange about it,' replied Surama, a little worked up. 'Have you ever taken any interest in what I do or don't do?'

Amar answered straightforwardly, 'I didn't until now. But since fate has brought Charu and me under your care, let's humbly accept the situation. Father selected you as the head of this household. I have no wish to remove you from that position, and I don't even feel I have the right to do so. You catered to everyone's comfort in this establishment. Continue to do so and leave Charu and me in peace.'

'Am I stopping you two from being at peace?'

'Not really. But you must look after the house. Do understand that you are the boss in this place just like before.'

Softly but clearly, Surama said, 'I do not understand.'

'What do you mean by that? Has anybody insulted you after my father's death?'

'No.'

'Return to your earlier role, then.'

'No,' said Surama again.

It was a small word but was loaded with meaning. It tore apart the façade that no rules needed to be changed after the zamindar's death. It somehow made Amar feel guilty and humiliated. His ears turned red and he felt his temper rise. 'Fine,' he said, proudly. 'Do as you please. I did not come here to beg for anything. I thought it was my duty to clear up any misconceptions you might have had.'

Surama said with a wry smile, 'Thank you for your selfless sense of duty.'

Amarnath stomped away.

Chapter 11

When Amarnath had left her room, Surama remained still for a while. Then, as if nothing had happened, she took out her wool, needle and fabric to resume her work on a small carpet, settling herself near the window again. She tried to concentrate on her work but her mind wandered. She remembered every detail of another meeting she had with her husband more than two years ago. That meeting had come to a bitter end. The discussion she just had with Amarnath ended in the same way. What a strange couple they were! 'Couple'—her lips curled into a smile of disdain. Yes, husband and wife—odd, but that was how they were.

So many months had passed, but every word that Amar had spoken to her on that fateful day remained crystal-clear in her mind. She had come to him in joyful expectation, unaware of the actual circumstances, only to be cruelly insulted. She was distressed for many days after that mortification. She relished the fact that it was he who had come now to make peace, well aware of the fact that she was a blessing and an asset to the family and that she was not to be belittled so easily. Humbly, he had requested her to take back what she had given up in wounded pride after he rejected her. The latest meeting with him was a kind of victory for her. And she wished she had the power to frustrate him even further.

Fatigued from her needlework and overwhelmed by her agitated mind, she left her piece of unfinished craft and came out on the veranda.

Below her was a yard surrounded by the kitchen, pantry and other rooms. Surama used to come here frequently to instruct the servants. After her withdrawal from work, she had stopped thinking of this place. Today, after Amar left her room, she was curious to see how things were downstairs.

Despite the evening setting in, she could discern what was happening below. The chaos both upset and pleased her. The newly appointed supervisor of provisions had gone away to take an evening break, keeping the storeroom locked. As a result, the cook did not have all the ingredients for his recipes, and the groom who had come to collect the daily quota of horse feed was stranded. The fish, sent from the ponds of the estate, were left to rot on the ground because the maid responsible for scaling and cutting them was quarrelling with someone else. When the butler tried to discipline the two and the other maids, one of them left her job then and there, saying, 'There is no justice here. There is nobody to see if people are getting a fair deal. How can one work in this place?' Surama wished that Amar, too, had watched the scene.

It was getting darker by the minute. Absent-mindedly, Surama paced back and forth on the veranda crossing Amar and Charu's room occasionally. Suddenly, she noticed a silhouette at the door of that room and thought that it must be Charu. As the figure left the door and moved towards her, Surama turned back and hurriedly came down to her own room. She was not in a mood to meet the younger woman, knowing that her words—whatever they may be—would fail to cheer her up.

When Surama awoke the next morning, bright daylight streaming through the windowpanes struck her eyes as soon as she opened them. 'Oh God, I have really overslept today,' she murmured and sat up. Then she remembered that she had nothing to do the whole day except for her needlework. She had shut herself in her room, confined herself to the bed, and had ordered the servants to not disturb her. As she remained seated with nothing to do and nothing to worry about, the sunny hour appeared quite cheerless to her.

She left the room and came out on the veranda. Standing next to a pillar, she pondered what could keep her busy for the rest of her life. The thought of not being engaged in meaningful activities made her feel wretched.

Downstairs, the maidservants had also woken up late. Two or three of them were yawning or rubbing their eyes. One of them was sitting on the ground with her legs stretched out, whining about the mosquitoes that bit her at night. Utensils, which had not been washed after last night's dinner, lay in a heap in a corner.

The sorry state of affairs perturbed Surama. Almost without realizing it, she shouted 'Bindi!' There was frantic activity and, in no time, all the servants were at their post. Bindi looked up and enquired if she should come upstairs.

'No. How sluggish all of you have become! Shame on you...' Surama heard footsteps and found that Amar was passing by. She felt terribly ashamed as she realized that her weakness—the desire to be in control—was exposed in Amar's presence. He, however, seemed quite indifferent to what she was doing.

Amar took the stairs to go down without pausing on his way. Hoping that Amar hadn't noticed her talking with the maids below, Surama strolled slowly on the veranda. Through the open door of Amar and Charu's room, she caught a glimpse of Charu still sleeping. She paused instinctively for a second before turning to go back. Just at that instant, she heard a faint moaning sound and saw Charu moving in her bed, whispering 'Mamma...'.

Surama stopped. Her sharp mind said, 'It sounds like she is not well. Should I go and check?' She reflected for a second. 'No, I won't. She has a husband to look after her. Who am I to worry? And I have other things to do. ...But what other things? Her husband passed me by just now, and he did not look concerned. Perhaps he does not yet know that the girl is ill. ...Yes, I must go and check on her. My conscience tells me to do that.'

Surama tiptoed inside the room and stood next to the large bed on which Charu lay with her eyes closed. Her face on the pillow looked like that of a sad child with signs of pain on her brow. Strands of dry, unkempt hair touched her cheeks. 'She is in pain,' whispered Surama to herself. 'O Mamma...' moaned the girl again. The next moment, she felt a cool hand on her forehead.

Charu opened her eyes. Her head had been aching and her eyes were closed as she thought of her mother. For an instant, she thought that her mother had come back from the dead. Looking again, she realized that it was not her mother but someone else with equally kind eyes. Then, recognizing Surama, she sat up on the bed. 'Didi...' she called. Catching hold of Surama's hand, she pulled her closer. When Surama took her seat on the bed next to her, Charu laid her head on the older woman's shoulder and called softly again, 'Didi!'

Charu's gesture of submission tugged at Surama's heartstrings. A helpless little one was looking up to her for protection. She felt like hugging Charu tightly but checked herself. Instead, she gently helped her lie back down on the bed. Then she touched her brow once more. 'You have a high fever. Is your head aching?' she asked.

'Yes, Didi, it is hurting badly.'

'Would you like me to massage it?'

'Yes, Didi. Please. Your hand has a cooling effect!'

After some time, Surama asked her, 'Since when are you having this fever?'

'I got it in the night. Before that, there was only a bad headache.'

'Why didn't you tell me, Charu? Why didn't you come to me?'

'When you were on the veranda last evening, I was coming to you. But you suddenly went away. Perhaps you remembered something that you needed to do. Perhaps you did not see me.'

Surama regretted walking away on seeing Charu.

'I *did* see you, Charu,' she said honestly, 'but still went away because…' She trailed off.

'Yes, Didi, you went away because you did not know, then, that I was ill. If you had known that, you would not have done so.'

In her mind, Surama said, 'Don't trust me so much, Child! Who knows what harsh words would have dropped from my lips if I had met you last evening. I was in a terrible mood then.'

Charu took hold of Surama's right hand and touched it to her temple. 'Ah, how cool and soft!'

'Is your head aching still?'

'Yes, Didi.'

'Maybe a few drops of eau de cologne would give you relief.' Surama got up to get a bottle of the freshener. She looked on the table, the shelf, and even in the glass showcase. Irritated, she said, 'Where have they disappeared? There were three or four bottles in this room!'

'Perhaps they have all been used up,' said Charu in a tired voice, raising her head from the pillow. 'There have been frequent headaches.'

'Who suffers from such headaches?'

'He does.'

'I see. But can't he replace the empty bottles with fresh ones? Quite an organized person he seems to be! Let me go and get a bottle of the freshener from elsewhere. I will ask Bindi to find one for me.'

'No, Didi, don't go. Your gentle hands are enough to make me well. Please don't go away, Didi.'

'Silly girl! Don't worry. I will come back in a minute.'

Surama left the room and came back with a small bottle of eau de cologne and a piece of cotton. She found Charu staring at the doorway expectantly, awaiting her return. Touched by Charu's welcoming look, Surama gave her a peck on the cheek, which made the younger girl smile from ear to ear. 'I was scared that you would not come back,' she said.

Surama needed a bowl or a tumbler to mix water and eau de cologne. She planned to use the ones she kept in the bedrooms, which were readily available. However, on this occasion, she discovered that the containers were missing from their assigned places. 'God knows where they have gone,' she murmured. There was a cupboard in the room which contained some crockery, but the key to open its panes was also not in its usual place. She called Charu for help, saying, 'Dear Charu, could you please hand me the keys? I need to open this almirah.'

'The keys, Didi? I don't know where they are. Maybe under this mattress.'

'Don't get up, Charu, I will look for it myself.'

Looking for the keys, Surama discovered how untidy and chaotic the room had become. It annoyed and angered her. And her anger was directed towards her husband. 'A good-for-nothing fellow!' she muttered under her breath. Unexpectedly, she felt a pang of sympathy for him in the next moment. She knew from her own life experience that one's efficiency could suffer when one's mind was not at peace.

It was easy enough to soothe Charu's forehead with the solution. The patient lay in bed, her forehead moistened from the soothing balm. Surama fanned her gently. 'Now, try to sleep,' she said. 'I have called the doctor. His medicine will help bring down your fever.'

'Will that be a bitter medicine, Didi? In Calcutta, Dr Naresh always prescribed bitter things for me.'

'No. This is Dr Kalipada. He is a homeopath, and his medicines are generally tasteless—like water. Now, be a good girl and sleep.'

Charu closed her eyes and tried to sleep as she had been instructed, but it eluded her.

'Didi, I can't sleep. Please, let's chat.'

'No, I don't think that is a good idea given your condition. Just tell me this: Doesn't he (Amar) know about your high fever?'

'I believe he doesn't. I only started feeling feverish late at night.'

'Did he not notice that you were running a temperature before he left in the morning?'

'I don't know. I was sleeping.'

'You've had a headache since yesterday afternoon. I suppose he was aware of that.'

'Yes, I remember him asking me how my head felt in the evening.'

'Was that all? I wonder how the two of you managed things in Calcutta. Who looked after you when either of you fell ill?'

'Tarini Dada mostly looked after us in Calcutta, but when I was seriously ill, even he (Amar) helped take care of me.'

'We've chatted enough. Try to sleep now.'

After a quiet spell, Charu fell asleep.

Surama heard footsteps on the veranda and, thinking they might be Amar's, quickly left the room through a side door that led to another room.

Amar had returned home on some errand. When he went to his bedroom, he was concerned to find Charu still asleep on the bed. On touching her, he discovered that she was burning with fever.

Just at that moment, a maid came in to announce that Dr Kalipada had arrived and was waiting outside the room.

Amar came out immediately and ushered in the doctor.

Feeling the sleeping Charu's pulse, the physician asked, 'Since when is she having this fever?'

'Can't say exactly. I suppose since last night. Shall we wake her up and ask her?'

'No need to do that. Though the temperature is high,

it does not indicate anything serious. Here are some tablets that must be given to her at regular intervals to bring down the fever. She will be fine. Don't worry. Just make sure that she takes her pills on time. I will take your leave now.'

A while after the doctor left, Charu woke up and called, 'Didi!'

Amar touched her brow and said, 'How hot you are!'

'When did you come back?' asked Charu.

'Just a short while ago. Why didn't you tell me you were ill, Charu?'

'I was asleep when you left in the morning. Who told you I was not well?'

'Nobody. When I came back, I found that you were asleep and running a fever. Just then, the doctor arrived to check on you. I didn't know you had summoned him.'

'I was not the one who called him.'

'Maybe some maidservant, seeing how ill you were, had sent for him. But you should have asked somebody to inform me that you were unwell.'

'Don't worry. Didi took care of me.'

'Which Didi?'

'Who else but my very own didi. She spent a long time with me. Wasn't she here when you came?'

'No. You were alone in the room.'

'She must have left before you came in.'

Surama, who was in the next room, heard Charu and blushed with embarrassment. She thought, 'That girl has no sense in her at all! Does she not realize that we must keep our interactions hidden from Amarnath? And shame on me for not instructing her about this beforehand.'

Chapter 12

Surama took care not to visit Charu that afternoon. When evening came, Charu begged Amarnath to send somebody to call Surama.

'Why? Do you need anything, Charu?' said Amar. 'I am here to attend to you. Just tell me if you need something.'

'Okay.'

Charu had no fever at night, and she slept well. In the morning, Amarnath said, 'You are quite recovered, Charu. So, I think I can leave you alone and go out. Read this book to pass your time. I will be back at ten to give you your next dose of medicine. Meanwhile, if you want anything, send me a message through a maid.'

Charu took up her book and tried to read, but she kept looking at the open door every little while, expecting somebody.

When she had gone through several pages of the book, she felt tired and achy. Putting the volume down, she surveyed the empty room. Then, she shouted at the top of her voice, 'Didi!'

Nobody came for a while. Then, Bindi, the maid, entered and asked, 'You called me, Little Boudidi?[8] Should I bring your barley drink now?'

Charu was slightly surprised that Bindi had sense enough

---

[8] In Bengali, 'boudidi' means wife of the master.

to prepare breakfast for her. But she said peevishly, 'No, I don't want anything. Please go away.'

'You should not starve yourself. Let me get the barley for you.'

'I am not hungry or thirsty. Leave me alone.'

Offended by Charu's rude words, Bindi left the room. Charu picked up her book and resumed reading. Her head had begun to ache. While she held the book in one hand, she massaged her temples with the other.

'Should one even read when one's head is aching?'

Charu looked up and found Surama standing near her bed, a bowl of gruel in her hand!

Instead of welcoming Surama, Charu held her book with both her hands and pretended to read. Seeing her sulk, Surama gently took the tome from her hands. 'Drink this, dear Charu. And, don't be so grumpy,' she said.

'I don't want it. I am not hungry.'

'It seems you are angry with somebody. We will deal with that later. First, drink your barley.'

This time, Charu sat up without any fuss and drank the beverage in one go.

'Now, tell me why you are so angry?'

Charu did not answer.

'Won't you tell me what is bothering you?' Surama asked her again. This time, Charu spoke up. 'Why haven't you come to see me since yesterday morning?'

'Oh, that's all! I thought something serious had cropped up.'

Charu was hurt that her reason for being upset was being belittled. Her large eyes filled with tears, which streamed down her cheeks despite her efforts to hold them back.

Surama was stunned. She cupped the face of her supposed rival with both hands, gazed into her eyes, and exclaimed, 'Did you really miss me that much?' Charu turned her face away and tried to wipe the tears.

Surama breathed heavily, and after spending a few moments in great amazement, sat beside Charu on the bed. She stared, vaguely, at the world outside the window and murmured to herself, 'Haven't seen anything like this before. Never imagined that this could happen!'

They were silent for a long time. Then, worried by Surama's grave expression, Charu softly called, 'Didi.' She asked, 'Are you very angry with me?'

Surama turned to Charu and spoke boldly, 'Yes, I am. Why are you trying to force me into an awkward situation? Don't you know who I am? Stop making a joke of our plight by playing this childish game. Is this the way you should behave?'

The harsh words terrified Charu. Her face turned ashen as she climbed out of the bed and stood on the floor, holding a poster to support her trembling body.

Surama cried out in awe, 'Charu, what happened?' She held the child-woman gently and lowered her back onto the bed. 'My little sister,' she whispered spontaneously. 'Okay, Charu, I won't scold you anymore. I am not a good person, you know.'

The kind tone in Surama's voice again brought tears to Charu's eyes. 'Just tell me, Didi, what have I done to offend you so much?'

'No, Charu. You have not done anything to offend me. I realize now that you are not capable of such a thing. It is entirely my fault. Who else can I blame for our unfortunate pairing?'

'I don't understand what you are speaking about.'

'Forget it. Just try to get some sleep.'

'But I know that you'll go away as soon as I fall asleep.'

'If I go away, I will come back again, later, as I have decided to spend more time with you. That will do me good; it will cleanse my mind. However, I shall be with you on one condition.'

'What condition, Didi?'

Surama paused for a few seconds. Then said, 'The condition is that you must not mention anything about me to your husband.'

'Why, Didi?'

'Whatever the reason, don't tell him about our interactions and the time we spend together.'

Charu agreed reluctantly. Then, after some thought, she asked, 'But, if he enquires about you?'

'Is he in the habit of enquiring about me?' asked Surama with a momentary flash in her eyes.

'No,' admitted Charu.

'Then relax,' said Surama. 'And, in case, he wants to know something about me or our time together, we will see what we need to tell him. I must leave you now.'

'Are you sure you have to go away now?'

'Yes, because your husband is about to come in.'

'What of that?'

'What of that? Have you already forgotten my agreement with you? There, I can hear him coming. I must go.' Surama opened the door leading to the next room.

'Please, Didi, what do I tell him if he wants to know if anybody had come to see me?'

'Don't tell him anything or tell him it was Bindi.' From the next room, Surama went to another, and soon found her way to another wing of the mansion.

⁂

'Whom were you speaking to?' asked Amar as he entered the room.

Charu kept quiet, hoping that he was not really interested in knowing.

'Are you feeling better, Charu? Your head isn't aching anymore, I hope. Should I call Bindi to keep you company?'

Charu was relieved that Amar was not too curious about what she was doing before he came in. She answered, 'Bindi, the maid? Okay, you may send her in.'

Shortly after Amar left the room, Bindi entered. 'You called me, Boudidi?' she asked. 'Do you need me to fan you?'

'No, Bindi. I just want you to sit with me and chat while Didi is away. Can you tell me where she is gone?'

'I guess in the kitchen or to the dining area.'

'I wonder when she will be back. Dear Bindi, please sit down and talk to me.'

'What do I talk about? I can recite some *shlokas*[9] for you. Want to listen?'

'No, Bindi. Tell me something about your village.'

'My village, Boudidi? Nothing interesting ever happens there. It would be better if you tell me about Calcutta. Doesn't Manikgunj feel dull to you after living there?'

'No, Bindi. I like this place better. In Calcutta, I had hardly anyone to talk to. There was nothing likeable in the city.'

---

[9]'Shlokas' are a type of Sanskrit verse or hymn that traditionally contain a concise message or principle.

'Such a big city with no people? Strange! Fortunately, we have no dearth of people in Manikgunj. For example, count the ladies who used to come to spend their free time in the afternoons. Under Elder Boudidi's hospitality, they used to have such fun. They played cards or just talked and laughed.'

'The ladies? I haven't seen any of them.'

'They have stopped coming since Elder Boudidi decided not to socialize.'

'But I would have enjoyed their company. Would have loved playing cards with them and Didi. Do you think, Bindi, they will come again if they are invited?'

'Of course, they would. They loved visiting this house and meeting Elder Boudidi.'

'And tell me, Bindi, do you all like your elder boudidi a lot? She is very fond of me, you know. I think she is a wonderful person.' Thus, unknowingly, Charu entered into Bindi's favourite topic. Bindi had a lot to say about her elder boudidi, whom she adored. So, she began with gusto.

'Yes, Boudidi, everybody respects her. You are a newcomer, but we know her since she came into this family as a bride. She is wise and kind. Our master, the zamindar, was very attached to her. He loved her like she was his real daughter. And she used to care for him with utmost sincerity. Nobody could have done as much for Master as she did...'

Bindi went on and on about Surama, and Charu listened with pleasure.

Charu had wanted to marry Amarnath, knowing full well that she would only be his second wife. Due to her naivety, she was unable to comprehend that this could even be an issue. In fact, she was happy at the prospect of gaining an 'elder sister' to share her life with. After coming to her marital home in Manikgunj, she was fascinated with Surama's multi-faceted personality. Charu had watched in amazement as Surama displayed her efficiency while nursing their father-in-law, handled all social interactions with dignity, and demonstrated her capacity for hard work. In her mind, Charu had placed Surama on a pedestal fit for a deity. When Haranath had joined the hands of his two daughters-in-law and asked Surama to take charge of Charu, the younger wife had happily submitted to her 'didi' in her mind.

Then, came the day of their father-in-law's demise. And, Surama, after completing her duties in connection with his last rites, went into retreat. She stopped taking any interest in the management of the household, and she stopped contacting Charu and Amarnath altogether.

Charu had been baffled. But when she had asked Amarnath if he knew the reason for Surama's behaviour, he refused to discuss the matter.

Charu was, therefore, overjoyed on getting back Surama's affectionate attention. Why? Till then, she herself was unaware that Didi could be *this* kind. Since she yearned to learn more about Surama, she relished every word spoken by Bindi.

Bindi spoke about a time when the zamindar of Manikgunj was alive and well. Under Surama's care, his household was a pleasant and peaceful place with all the warmth of an ideal home. Charu did not have any recollection of her own father as she was too small when he died. She was mesmerized by Bindi's account of Surama and Haranath's close bond, as she had never experienced the tenderness and affection of a father–daughter relationship. Charu recognized Surama as the dominant figure in the beautiful setting described by Bindi. In that moment, her reverence for her didi surged, and she felt immensely proud that the same meritorious woman had been especially kind to her since the previous day. 'You know, Didi is very fond of me, too!' she repeated.

Amarnath entered the room at that moment, putting an end to Bindi's narration. Bindi stood up, put the fan in its place, and took her leave.

'Good,' said Amarnath, 'it looks like you got along well with Bindi.'

'Yes, we were talking about Didi.'

Usually, Amarnath became uncommunicative whenever Charu made any reference to Surama. This time, however, he blurted out, 'Is that such a great topic for storytelling?'

'Bindi was not telling me stories; she was relating facts about Didi. She was telling me how everyone adores her.'

'I see.'

'Do you know that Baba was very fond of her? He loved her as if she were his own daughter.'

'Yes, I know that.'

'Didi, who looked after the house and oversaw several activities of the estate, stopped visiting her own father. Her father came to take her home several times, but she refused to go. She didn't want things to fall apart here.'

Amar said, 'With her inclination for fantasy, Bindi would have done better if she had related genuine fairy tales and ghost stories to you. It would have been better if she had entertained you with stories about poor giants and demons, who were asked to carry out impossible tasks!'

Despite Amar's teasing comment, Charu went on, 'And, Bindi said that Didi is always kind to the staff. She has a knack for accounting. She was Baba's account-keeper for all his expenses.'

Amarnath smiled, trying to look amused. 'It seems you know her better than I do. However, I have found her to be just the opposite of what you say.'

'Just the opposite? How come?' Charu was surprised.

'Now, tell me how you feel. Not feverish, again, I hope?'

'I am quite well today. But, please tell me what you know about Didi.'

'Let it be. I don't feel like talking about it now. Tell me, how much did you read?' Picking up the book that Charu had been reading, Amar flipped through it.

'Oh dear, you are trying to change the subject! Do tell me what you dislike about Didi.'

Without looking up from the book, Amar began, 'She doesn't care for us. She thinks all her responsibilities towards this family ended with Baba's death. She had stopped looking after the house, and things were getting out of hand. On Shyamacharan Kaka's advice, I met her and urged her to take over the management again, but...' Amar stopped.

'But what?'

'You are too young to grasp the nuances of our conversation, but the gist of it is that she doesn't want to cooperate with me in any of my affairs.'

Though Charu was appalled by the revelation, she made an effort to not let that tarnish her favourable impression of Surama. She said, 'Nevertheless, Didi is very fond of me.'

Amar did not know what to say. He found it weird how Charu insisted on speaking well of Surama. Her statement sounded like something mistakenly uttered in the wrong context. 'Maybe,' he said wryly.

Charu did not notice Amar's distaste for the subject. She went on, enthusiastically, 'She massaged my brow when I was in pain. So, soothing her touch was! I put my head on her lap and slept. When I woke up, my pain was gone. I love her.'

Amar could not help being amazed. What he thought would be impossible was actually happening here! What was playing out seemed like a tale from *The Arabian Nights*. He forced himself to let out a laugh. 'I know you, Charu. Anybody, even I, could easily pretend to love you.'

'Oh, no. I am not that silly. Do you think I cannot tell when someone truly loves me?'

Amar sighed. 'You are a blessed creature, Charu,' he said. 'You will never be unhappy in life because you can draw people close to your heart effortlessly.'

'You still think I am a simpleton? Now, hear this. I have something complex to tell you: I know that Didi is not very pleased with you because she said…'

This time, really amused, Amarnath laughed heartily. 'A unique discovery, Charu! I have to say you have brains.'

'Don't make a joke out of it. Let me tell you what Didi said.' At this point, Charu suddenly remembered the promise of secrecy given to Surama. That she could not keep her word even for a day filled her with remorse.

Finding her quiet, Amar prompted her to proceed. 'What did she say about me?'

'No, I won't tell you. I know Didi will not like me to share it with you.'

Chapter 13

Hurt by Surama's refusal to look after his household and not being able to manage things himself, Amarnath called Tarani from Calcutta. He had great faith in Tarini's ability to set things right.

Taking advantage of his high position as Amarnath's brother-in-law, Charu's cousin took matters into his own hands. But he was a ruthless and uncaring taskmaster. As a result, employees of the estate and members of Amar's extended family who lived with him were at their wits' end.

When things were in such a state, Surama learnt one morning that the diwan had resigned. Taking his leave from Amar, he had left for Varanasi. He had intentionally avoided meeting Surama before going away.

Surama was stunned, realizing that she could not remain an uninvolved bystander any longer if she wanted to prevent the Mitra family from sinking into ruin.

In another part of the mansion, a greatly agitated Amarnath, wondering how to fill the void left by Shyamacharan, came to consult Tarini, who said with a nonchalant air, 'There's nothing to worry about, Amar Babu. A diwan's work will be easy for me to handle. I just need to sack the whole bunch of old veterans from the estate office. Indulged for years, they have become a nuisance now.'

Not really convinced by Tarini's words, Amar murmured his assent hesitantly, 'Hmm'.

When Tarini arrived at work to take over as the manager the next morning, he was met with a surprise: on every important document, Surama's signature as the CEO of the zamindari stood out.

Enraged, he rushed to Amarnath and reported the 'ridiculous development'. 'I suppose I am not required here anymore,' he said, grudgingly. But Amar's reaction was the opposite of what Tarini had expected. 'Is this true?' Amar enquired excitedly. 'Has she taken over? Ah, what a relief!'

Tarini's face flushed with disgust.

'Believe me, Tarini,' Amar said, 'what is happening is a good thing. Looking after this estate would have been a huge challenge for any inexperienced person. Moreover, the work will include the management of a large house. And, what do we, men, know about housekeeping? It needs a woman's involvement.'

Offended, Tarini looked sullen.

∞

Over the next few months, the family enjoyed a period of peaceful existence. Despite Tarini's attempts to avoid Surama, she somehow managed to guide him in every important transaction of the estate.

Amarnath, who had opened a charitable nursing home on the premises of his property, spent long hours treating patients for free.

Surama restrained herself from speaking hurtful words to Amar, though she avoided meeting him except when it was necessary to discuss important matters related to their zamindari. She and Charu continued to get along wonderfully as always. Mentoring Charu, along with her other duties, kept Surama fully occupied.

The earnings from the family's holdings showed a steady rise.

Amar was not blind to Surama's abilities. A woman who could save a major establishment from certain doom with just a glance of her benevolent eye was certainly deserving of respect. Amarnath developed a genuine respect for Surama. He felt ashamed when he remembered how vastly mistaken he had been about her even a few months back.

Chapter 14

Five and a half years passed in comparative peace for the Mitras.

With an effort, Surama had taught herself to interact with Amar as if he were just a friend. Amarnath had not honoured her claims as a wife. Surama, who had her pride, was determined to show him that she did not care.

Charu and Amar's son, four-year-old Atul, had won her heart, and Charu remained, as before, a kid sister for her to play with and to take care of. In business matters and managing the household, she assisted Amar as an efficient colleague. During his moments of enjoyment and fun, she joined in as a good-humoured and witty participant. Her pleasant expression gave everyone the impression that she was happy. Charu had devoted herself to Surama out of the goodness of her heart, and even Amar had become comfortable around her.

But one evening, Surama was sitting alone in her room. Some days back, she had received from her father the sad message that his only son, a stepbrother of Surama, had passed away. Surama now was her father's only living child.

Surama knew how deeply distressed her father would be to have lost a son who was also designated as his heir. Her heart went out to her grieving father.

Charu entered the room and called, 'Didi! What are you doing all alone?'

'Where is Atul, Charu?'

'He is sleeping. Didi. Let's go up to the terrace and chat for a while.'

While they were talking, Amar came and stood at the door. Noticing him, Surama said, 'There, somebody else to make sure I am not left alone.'

They went to the terrace and chatted for a while.

※

The next evening, the family had a special guest. Surama's father, Zamindar Radhakishore, had come to take her home.

After a long tête-à-tête with his daughter, Radhakishore left for the guesthouse in the outer quarters of the Mitras' residence.

Entering Surama's room, Charu found her deep in thought. 'What have you decided, Didi?' asked an anxious Charu.

'I must go, Charu. He needs me.'

'I know it is your duty to be with him. But will you be able to part with Atul?'

'What can I not do, Charu? Don't you know that I am a weird and cold person?'

'Didi, you never stop teasing me, even when you have serious things to think about. When have I called you 'cold', Didi? Don't I know how kind-hearted you are?'

Amar had entered the room, but seeing the two women engrossed in intimate conversation at the other end of the spacious chamber, he waited at the door. Looking at him, Surama said jokingly, 'Is that a spy keeping a watch on us?'

'A spy to be sure,' said Amar, good-humouredly, 'but quite inefficient. He is still ignorant of the latest news. So, what have you decided?'

'Will go with him.'

'But Father wishes to return this evening itself.'

'I will get ready by then.'

Amar hesitated a little before asking, 'For how long are you going to be there?'

The query triggered a sudden bout of harshness in Surama. Her bright eyes met Amar's as she said, 'Can't say. Could be forever.'

Charu hugged Surama and said plaintively, 'Don't say that, Didi!'

What she had heard from her father was still preying on Surama's mind and had made her bitter. As gently as he could, Zamindar Radhakishore had disclosed to his daughter what relatives and acquaintances were talking about in her absence. How shameful was Surama's attachment to a husband who had rejected her for his second wife, they said.

After caresses to Atul, loving gestures to Charu, and business advice to Amar—Surama left for Kaligunj with her father that night.

Charu found it very difficult to manage Atul in Surama's absence. Amar had to lend her as much assistance as he could. He stopped hunting and reduced his visits to his nursing home.

Atul was a hyperactive child and a picky eater. Surama was the only person who could coax him to have his daily quota of milk. At bedtime, Atul would begin to cry for his Ma, Surama, and pacifying him would be difficult. Unable to see the child suffering, Amar would go up to the terrace and sit alone, leaving Charu to manage things.

After a few trying weeks, Charu proposed, 'Please go and get Didi back.'

'Ask me to do anything, Charu, except that,' said Amar.

'What else can you do for me?' asked Charu.

'What else? Really? Have you already forgotten what I have done for you?' exclaimed Amar in mock anger. 'Don't forget that I am an older friend of yours than your Didi.'

Chapter 15

Months passed. It irritated Amar that Charu was still pining for Surama. One day, when he was about to tell Charu that he had finalized a plan for a family holiday in a resort in the neighbouring western state of Bihar, and she must get ready for that, Charu, happy and excited, came to call him, 'Come and see what I am capable of achieving.'

'What do you mean?'

'I have brought Didi back.'

'Really?'

'Come and see for yourself.'

Amar followed Charu and entered a room where little Atul and Surama were having their reunion. The five-year-old child was overwhelmed with feelings of joy and anger. He was angry that his Ma had taken so long to come back from wherever she had gone to. Surama was trying to calm him down with various explanations while he wept.

Amar stood nearby and watched. Though he wanted to say something light-hearted to Surama, he found himself unable to speak.

Charu said, 'Leave Atul alone, Didi, and attend to me. I am angry, too. We all are.'

'I hardly care about your anger, Charu,' said Surama with a smile.

'Never mind,' said Charu. 'But what about the other person?'

'Not too worried about that because...'

Before she could finish her sentence, Amar said, 'Angry for what? Am I out of my mind to get angry with you for doing what you thought was your duty? But wasn't your father displeased with you for wanting to come back here?'

'He was, initially, but I explained to him how this household needed me more than his. Anyway, he did bless me when I took my leave. I advised him to adopt a male heir.'

Amar's eyes widened, 'You went that far? Was it the right thing to do?'

'What else could I do when people wanted me here?'

'I never did. I never asked you to sacrifice your prospects or personal interests.'

'Sorry. I did not express myself well. I came back because Charu wrote to me again and again, saying she wanted me here.'

'Why didn't you ignore her?'

'I didn't think of ignoring her. Her appeals were very precious to me. But, if you don't like me to live here, I will go back immediately.'

'Stay!' said Amar. Then, after a brief pause, he continued, 'I would have advised you to go back if I were really interested in your well-being. I know how, by choosing to come here, you are even ready to give up your claim to your father's huge property. But...'

'But what?'

'But you know how I believe that everybody is selfish in this world. If Charu and I want you to be here for our selfish needs, we won't be committing a crime that the world is unused to.'

Charu said, 'Enough of your philosophical ramblings for now. I am taking Didi for a wash-up and rest.'

Within a few days, the family found itself in its previous rhythm. However, soon troubles appeared. Amar was unable to manage the zamindari effectively in Surama's absence—a weakness Tarini exploited for his own gain. Tarini's misadventures led to several court cases.

So, a distraught Amarnath spent all his waking hours trying to set things right. But matters were too far gone. The Basus, who were the perpetual rivals of the Mitras, had covertly bribed Tarini to side with them in the ongoing disputes between the two zamindaris. Moreover, disgusted with Tarini's ill-treatment, the tenants of several plots of the Mitras' land had stopped paying their dues. They even blamed the Mitras for one or two murders that had taken place in their areas. Amar's money was spent like flood waters to pay the lawyers, barristers and witnesses. Things came to such a pass that it looked like he would have to surrender parts of his property to pay the compulsory land tax to the government. Neither Surama nor Amar knew how to tide over the crisis. In desperation, Surama advised Amar to send a telegram to Shyamacharan Roy in Varanasi.

Shyamacharan arrived in a few days and said, 'Won't you release this old man even to let him die in peace?'

'No, Uncle, we have discovered that we cannot live without you looking after us,' said Amar and Surama.

∞

Crisis followed crisis. Atul contracted typhoid fever and fell seriously ill. Shyamacharan said to Surama, 'Dear Child, I know how busy you will be with Atul now. Don't worry about business. I will do my best to deal with it and see what Fate holds for us.'

Surama appointed herself as Atul's principal nurse. Caring for the little patient, she forgot to sleep and even forgot to eat and drink. The most famous doctor in the region was called in to treat the boy, but days passed without any improvement in his condition. Eventually, Atul was on the verge of death.

Charu was too naïve to understand the gravity of the situation. She would look at the patient's gaunt face and ask Surama, 'Will he recover, Didi?'

'Why not?' Surama would reply promptly to set Charu's mind at ease.

One night, however, the boy's condition became really worrisome. He was struggling to breathe and experiencing distress throughout his body. Surama summoned Amar, who was sleeping in the next room. Setting his eyes on his son, Amar realized how bad his condition was. 'Call, Charu. We cannot keep her in the dark anymore,' urged Surama. 'She entrusted me with her jewel, but I have proved unworthy of her confidence in me. Let him go back to his mother now.'

'Don't give up,' said Amar. 'God would not like to be so unkind to you. Not for Charu or me, perhaps, but for your sake, He might allow Atul to live. Trust in Him. Let Charu sleep.'

Amar's encouraging words overwhelmed Surama, who clutched his hands in sudden excitement. With wide eyes, she said, 'Will He? Are you sure? Atul will not be taken away from me? Your words give me hope again.'

'I strongly believe in what I said.'

Surama steadied herself and softly called the boy, 'Atul!' There was no answer.

It was well past midnight. The two adults kept a watch over the sick child. Towards dawn, he seemed slightly better. He was sleeping with a regular heartbeat. Amar took his temperature and found it had come down two degrees. Surama sighed in relief. 'Dear God,' she said, 'thank you for giving this sweet relief to Atul.'

Amar said, 'Why don't you get some sleep, Surama? You can rely on me to keep a watch on Atul.'

'No, no!' exclaimed Surama. 'I cannot leave his side now. I cannot relax if I leave him with anybody else. Wonder how Charu does that!'

'That is the reason why Charu is happy. I believe Trust is the root of happiness.'

Amar left the room after a while, but Surama continued to sit next to the patient. Soon, it was morning.

'Listen,' said Amar when he entered the sickroom next, 'I have decided to treat the patient myself from now on with whatever skill I have. Obviously, the regular medicines have not worked for him. A month has gone by, and he has only become worse.'

'I agree. Go ahead and give him your medicines. I, too, have lost faith in our doctor.'

There was a general belief that medical practitioners should avoid treating their kin, as they were not expected to be objectively detached enough for such situations. But Atul showed signs of improvement with his father's medicines. In a few days, his temperature became normal. His parents and Surama breathed a sigh of relief. But the kid remained very weak, needing constant attention in bed, even at night.

Charu said, 'Didi, let me look after him for a few days. I know how tired and strained you are after nights without sleep. You need some rest. If you fall ill yourself, it will be a calamity for us.'

'Why will it be a calamity, Charu? Won't you be able to nurse me to health in a jiffy?'

'Can't guarantee that,' joked Charu, 'when I compare my nursing skills with yours.'

Surama smiled and said, 'Nothing will happen to me, I assure you. Let me attend to Atul for a few more days. Now, you go to sleep like a good girl. You, too, need to rest.'

Obedient as ever, Charu did as she was told.

Atul woke up in the middle of the night and called, 'Ma!'

'Here I am, Atul,' said Surama. She lifted the child onto her lap and gave him a few sips of pomegranate juice to drink. Satisfied, he raised his thin hand to Surama's shoulder and gently hugged her. 'Sleep, Shona,' said Surama as she rocked him slowly. The boy fell into a peaceful sleep, holding his stepmother's hand.

Surama had been working with nervous energy and was sleep-deprived for one and a half months. Now, satisfied that Atul was better, she could hardly keep her eyes open. Resting her back against the wall, she closed her eyes and fell into a deep slumber. Who knows for how long she remained sitting in that manner? The sensation of somebody lifting Atul out of her lap awakened her. 'Who is it?' asked Surama and found that it was Amar.

'I will put Atul in bed. No point in staying awake unnecessarily. You look very tired. Go to sleep,' said Amar.

Surama had no strength to resist. She lay down where she was, and before she was fast asleep, felt somebody holding her head and putting it gently on the pillow.

Surama slept like a corpse till late in the morning. 'Didi,' called Charu, 'do get up now. I know you don't want to miss your morning puja.'

'My God! How late it is! How could I sleep this long?'

'I am sure you cannot be blamed for that,' said Charu in amusement.

'How is Atul?'

'Better. Is speaking like he always does. Has eaten Millins[10] food a few times.'

'I was unaware of everything. Was sleeping like Kumbhakarna.[11] At night, did you carry Atul from my lap?'

'No, not I. Probably, he did. He was watching over Atul at night while you slept. He asked me not to disturb you.'

Surama was embarrassed to learn that Amar was sitting so close to her when she was oblivious to her surroundings. But there was nothing she could do about it. So, she tried to ignore the sensation of awkwardness in her mind.

Atul continued to gain strength as days passed and everybody expected him to be healthy again soon. In the meantime, Shyamacharan Roy had been able to set right the affairs of the zamindari. When the full extent of Tarini's deceit came to light, Shyamacharan wanted to hand him over to the police. But Amar had pleaded with Shyamacharan, 'Please, Uncle, let us not go that far. Sacking him immediately will be punishment enough for him.'

So, after an ugly exchange of words, Tarini left Manikgunj.

---

[10]A baby food brand of that era.
[11]One of Ravana's brothers in the Ramayana. He slept six months in a year.

A curious change came over Amar. Surama noticed that he had lost interest in activities close to his heart—running his nursing home and going for hunts. And yet, he was away from home most of the day. As the days went by, his easy-going, fun-filled interactions with Charu came to a stop and he spoke less and less with Surama. It seemed he was desperate to avoid any closeness with Surama. He tried to remain away from her as much as possible. Sometimes, when Surama spoke to him, he pretended not to hear. What could have happened? Surama was worried. Did the peculiar change have a psychological trigger or was it a symptom of ill-health? The former seemed more likely to Surama. But what could have made him lose attraction to Charu? If it were any other man, Surama could have suspected that he had a tainted character. But she was aware of how devoted a husband Amar was to Charu. She was sure that no other woman could come between the two. And yet...

One day Amar said to Charu, even in the presence of Surama, 'I don't feel too well these days, Charu. I think a change of place will do me good. Why don't we three—Atul, you and I—go for a vacation? Remember, I was planning for a holiday even before Atul fell ill?'

'And Didi?' asked Charu, surprised. 'Won't she come with us?'

'No. Shyamacharan Uncle will need somebody from the family to stay back.'

'Then, let us not go at all.'

'Don't behave like a child, Charu!' scolded Surama. 'I think it is a very good idea for you three to have a break. It will help Atul regain his strength faster.'

'And you will be all alone here?'

'I won't be alone. Uncle is here. And there are other people in the house.'

However, Charu carried on in the same vein. Addressing Amar, she said, 'Please ask Didi to come along with us.'

'No,' said Amar. 'I don't want things to get complicated.'

Charu stared at him in disbelief. What did those strange words mean? Was he stricken by some sudden disorder of the mind? Yes, the glow in Amar's eyes seemed to suggest that. Really worried for her husband, Charu said softly, 'Do whatever will be good for you.'

⁂

The very next day, Amar, Charu and Atul left for the tourist destination in Bihar with only a manservant and a maidservant.

Before leaving, a teary-eyed Charu took Surama's blessings, saying, 'I wonder what Fate holds for us, Didi. Do wish Atul and his father good health.' Surama gently caressed Charu's cheek and tenderly kissed Atul's forehead. 'I am your elder sister who will never cease to bless you,' she thought.

They had to drag a crying Atul, who did not want to leave, to the car. Surama stood and watched them till their faces in the moving vehicle disappeared. She went straight to her room after that and shut herself in. When she opened the door after several hours, night had descended. The darkness deepened the void inside her. She yearned for something, however small and insignificant, to call her own, but could think of nothing. She felt as if she had used up all her savings while there was no income. In her life's account book, she entered a zero as her balance.

Amarnath had rented a small but picturesque bungalow

on a hillock in Mungher to spend his holiday with Charu and Atul. The River Ganges washed the foot of the hillock while just above, skirting the bungalow, was a charming garden. Impressed with his new living quarters, Amar breathed a sigh of relief. Unwanted longings had been left behind in an ordinary bedroom in a humdrum village in Bengal to die a natural death. In the new surroundings, he would live like a free bird. To celebrate his freedom, he took a long swim in the Ganges every morning, joyously splashing water around him. In the evenings, he took his wife and son out to visit tourist spots in the city: Pir Pahar, Sita Konda, Karan Chuda or the fort. That her husband was happy made Charu happy, too, and of course, she was thrilled to discover a new place. Though there was no time for Charu to give special attention to Atul, the salubrious air of the region helped the child to recoup faster.

By and by, the novelty of Mungher wore off. 'When are we going back?' Charu asked Amar.

'What's the hurry?'

'But, for how long are we going to be here?'

'For as long as we want to.'

'Please, let us go back. I feel homesick.'

'Will think about it. Bear with me for a few more months. And, dear Charu, check my forehead to see if it is warm.'

'It is burning!' said Charu on touching Amar's brow. 'Why do you take such long baths in the Ganges?'

'Did not expect to get a fever. I have a bad headache, too. Won't have anything for dinner tonight. Be careful with Atul.'

In the morning, Amar took his own temperature and found it to be 104 degrees. He had a severe body ache and chest pain, too.

'I am quite unwell, Charu,' said Amar. 'Do send for a doctor. And send a telegram home, asking Shyamacharan Uncle to come over as it will be too difficult now for you to manage alone.'

Charu began to cry. 'Why didn't you bring Didi with us? What will happen to us now? Even Atul seems to be feverish today.'

'Is that so? What a confounded situation!'

'Let me send a telegram to Didi, asking her to come here immediately.'

'No, no. You shouldn't do that!' said Amar, emphatically.

Surprised, Charu stared at Amar's flushed features. 'What has happened to you? Don't you realize that we cannot do without her in such a situation? I will ask her to come.'

'No, Charu, please. Won't you be able to look after me? I know you will be. You are a brave girl. Let only Uncle come over.'

'Okay. As you wish. Don't talk so much.'

'I won't. It's getting difficult for me to talk or even to think clearly.'

The doctor diagnosed Amar's illness as typhoid. He advised him to take complete rest and other precautions. With proper care, he expected the invalid to recover.

At eight in the morning, the sound of a car could be heard at the gate. Charu broke into a run, calling, 'Didi!'. However, when she saw Shyamacharan getting out of the vehicle, she covered her head and halted respectfully.

Surama came out of the car next. 'Didi!' called Charu, again, her voice choking with emotion.

'Have you left him alone in the room, Charu?' asked Surama.

'No, the maid is there.'

'Good.'

Shyamacharan entered the patient's room. Charu hugged Surama. 'What will happen to us, Didi?'

'He will get well soon. Come, let's see how he is doing now.'

'But won't you have to freshen up after your journey? Don't you need your breakfast?'

'I will find time for all that. Don't worry. Bindi has come with us. Ask her to arrange for Uncle's food and bathing. You look terribly tired, Charu. If you don't get some sleep, you won't be able to stand up.'

Relieved to hand over her charge to her didi, Charu obeyed.

Amar lay in distress, moaning and tossing in bed.

'Shall I massage your brow?' asked Surama.

'Who is speaking?' asked Amar, startled. 'Are you Surama?'

'Yes.'

'When did you come?'

'I came just now, with Shyamacharan Uncle.'

Amar felt excited by Surama's sudden presence, but it soon transformed into a feeling of tranquillity. 'I thought you won't come.'

'Why?'

Amar did not answer. Though he didn't say it in words, his facial expression conveyed the feeling that Hope and Trust were visiting him in person. 'Has Charu met you?' he asked.

'Yes.'

Amar closed his eyes and murmured, as if just to himself,

'I will get better now.' Surama did not comment, but went on gently caressing Amar's feverish forehead.

The doctor came for his visit soon. There was no reason to panic, he said. But the nature of the fever would make the patient suffer for some time, he added.

Surama, as was her nature, sat with the patient day and night, forgetting to eat, drink or sleep. She appealed to Charu not to neglect Atul at all costs. So, Charu spent most of her time with her little son while Bindi attended to the needs of the others.

Soon, Amar was on the path of recovery. Shyamacharan met Surama one day to say, 'If you allow me, Child, I will go back to Manikgunj now. As you know, our coming here at short notice has left many things disorganized back home. They need my attention. Amar's health is improving. And you are taking excellent care of him. So, I don't need to be here anymore.'

Both Surama and Amar agreed that the diwan was urgently needed at home and granted his wish.

After making proper arrangements to ensure that the family's Mungher establishment ran smoothly, Shyamacharan left for Manikgunj.

Though Amar was on the mend, he was too weak to leave his bed for too long in the initial stages of his convalescence. Charu kept busy with Atul and her household, managing to be with Amar only occasionally. As was her wont, she had put all her faith in Surama for bringing Amar out of his weakened state. Moreover, she knew how clumsy she was in the matter of nursing the sick and so, did not want to be in the way of Surama's work.

Away from home, in a rented bungalow, Amar's loneliness

was lessened only by Surama's bright presence. She was not only his nurse but also his assistant and companion.

A convalescent often becomes hungry for love and sympathy. He may become more emotionally attuned to sensing love and affection from others. Someone's interest in him, which he might have been too careless to observe, comes to his notice quickly in his weakened state. And, love grows in his heart, in return, like a seed suddenly getting moisture in otherwise barren soil. In no time that seed of love sprouts into a sapling, then, grows into a tree with branches and leaves. Amid the rat race of everyday life, regard and appreciation for a deserving fellow-being often remain unexpressed. During a period of convalescence, when one may feel dependent and weak, feelings of admiration for another may intensify, like a hundred streams seeking to drench the object of one's affection. And one may feel a humble desire to express one's need to be wanted and loved. A convalescent is as keen to receive love as he is to give it.

It was evening. The breeze that came through the open window filled the room with a faint floral scent. Amarnath was lying on one end of the large bed, while Surama was sitting at the other end, busy writing something.

Suddenly, the open windows came to her notice. 'Oh God, it is already eight and I haven't shut the windows!' exclaimed Surama. She was about to get down from the bed to shut them when Amar held her hand. 'Let them remain open for a while longer. Such sweet fragrance is coming from outside,' he said. 'Come, tell me some stories.'

'Stories? About what?'

'Anything except tigers and jackals.'

'I hardly know any stories except those about them. Want to hear some,' Surama joked.

'No, actually, I want to hear some serious stories. ...I know you have received a letter from your dad today. What has he written?'

'Many things. It's a long letter. For him, I am still a child. He has written it as if he is writing to a small girl. He has ended it by saying that he is still waiting for me to go back to him—that he would wait for me until I make up my mind.'

'Have you made up your mind?'

'Not yet. What is your advice?'

'Write to him that you can't go.'

Surama laughed and said, 'What a childish thing to say! How can a fit person like me, with hands and legs in order, say that she can't go?'

'I strongly feel you can't go. You won't go. Something inside me says that.'

Surama got up from her seat quickly. 'Don't depend on such vague feelings. You could be totally wrong.' She got busy in closing the windows.

After a few weeks, when Amar was doing quite well, Surama proposed, 'Let's all go back to Manikgunj.'

'Why the hurry?' asked Amar.

'Perhaps you are not in a hurry. But I am. Let me go back, then.'

'Why are you so keen to go back?'

'Just like that.'

'It is not "just like that". I know what it is.'

'You do?'

'Yes.'

'What is it?'

'You don't like the way I behave with you these days.'
'Could be.'
'Don't shrug it off. Tell me what you don't like in what I do.'

Those were simple words but spoken with such appeal that Surama could not respond to them at once.

Amar continued, 'You may think that I haven't noticed. But I have. I have noticed your embarrassment. But, I have this much to say: What's the harm if we enjoy our recent closeness? Why do you feel so uncomfortable about it?'

Surama decided that she must not keep quiet any longer. 'Have you gone mad?' she asked.

Amar came forward and held her hand. 'Yes, I have,' he said. 'And I want an answer from you. Don't I deserve even the intimacy due to a distant relative?'

Surama pulled her hand out of Amar's grasp. With a raised chin and a steady gaze, she said firmly, 'No, you do not deserve even that. To me, you are the most disconnected outsider I have ever come across. Don't you know that when a relationship breaks, the partners are torn apart forever? They are divided by a gulf wider than that between the most distant relatives. I am kind to you, I know. But that is only for the sake of Charu and Atul. They are all that I have. You are nothing to me.'

'I know how the situation is. Even so...can I not expect anything from you? Am I not entitled to even the smallest consideration? No matter how terrible a sinner I may be, there's no denying that we are married. So, don't I have the right to... No, no, I am not speaking of my rights. But can't I expect from you the merest tenderness, the merest closeness that any human being owes to a casual acquaintance?'

'No, you are not fit even for that. Charu is the only reason for my being concerned about you. I had tried to remove myself from this family once. Didn't you realize that? But Charu did not let me leave in peace. I had to come back for her sake. And you? There is no one in this universe as unrelated to me as you are.'

Though Amar was deeply distressed, he did not move away from her presence at once. In fact, he was about to plead with her once more. However, Surama snubbed him by leaving the room.

She found a secluded place in the building to reflect. What strange plans did destiny have for her? Once upon a time, years ago, her trusting, youthful heart had met with a terrible rebuff from her man. For many months thereafter she had tried to hurt him in return—experimenting with various methods—but had failed. He had remained stubbornly indifferent to her feelings. By and by, she had learnt to live with the facts. She had taught herself to feel kindly towards him without expecting anything in return. Suddenly, she finds him changed! The longings of her earlier, adolescent spirit, tortured by Amar's ill-treatment, had, long ago, moved to a hiding place deep inside her inner self. Somebody was knocking at its door, unexpectedly, asking her to open it. That 'somebody' was Amar, who could have been her man but was not anymore. For, he was her dearest sister's husband—entitled only to the kindness due to a brother-in-law. What kind of an enigma was that?

Charu had a right over Surama's heart. For, was not she her younger sister? And Amar was now that younger sister's husband. How can she ever fall for him? Surama reddened from head to foot at the idea.

The next instant, it occurred to Surama that Charu could have understood that Amar now longed for her didi. It should be terrible if she did so! Surama having an affair with Charu's husband? She wiped some sweat off her brow. Amar was Charu's man and, she, Surama, did not have any right to be resentful towards him. She wished to have only good feelings for Charu's husband and, so far, had been almost successful in including him in the arc of her affection, where Atul and Charu belonged. Then, why was she so filled with disgust? What a nuisance was this! Her love for Charu's family was so very stable and firm until this sudden attack on it by Amar. Now, Charu might even begin to suspect it to be Surama's doing—imagining Surama to be the instigator, the temptress! Surama laid herself on the carpet she was sitting on and covered her face with her hands. Shame, shame, shame!

What was to be done now? The thought worked on her like an animal tearing her insides. Should she run away? But, what if Charu had already inferred something from Amar's recent behaviour? Surama's departure would make her more suspicious. It could even suggest to Charu's mind something worse than what had really happened. Leaving the family was, therefore, out of the question. Surama had to deal with the problem by staying on.

She fell asleep long after midnight but continued to grapple with the situation in her nightmares. On waking up, Surama decided that the problem was too complex. She couldn't deal with it by continuing to stay there. She had no choice but to leave the family, whatever Charu might make of that.

Chapter 16

A day came when the whole family was back in Manikgunj. And soon the news spread that Surama was leaving for her father's home. People guessed that she was going away for good. The diwan asked, 'Why, Child?'

'Why not, Uncle,' said Surama with a smile. 'I thought it proper to claim my inheritance so that I can give it to Atul.'

Shyamacharan realized how determined Surama was to go, and so, desisted from urging her to do otherwise. But, with a sigh, he said to Amarnath, 'It seems I have to give up my idea of spending my last days in Kashi (Varanasi).'

'Dear Uncle, please don't worry,' said Amarnath. 'I have learnt to look after the zamindari now. So, I won't hold you back. I have no right to stop you from doing what you wish to. Let everybody fulfil their wishes.'

Charu hugged Surama and wept without saying a word. Surama, with tears in her own eyes, said, 'Charu, my sister, I am sorry to be leaving you. But, please understand... Please don't make me sad.'

'I didn't know you could be so cruel, Didi.'

'Dear Charu, please don't call me that. I cannot bear to hear that from *you*. Let people all over the world call me names. I don't care. But it hurts me when *you* are angry with me.'

'Then, Didi, stay here for me.'

'Please do not ask me to do that for I won't be able to oblige you.'

Coming to Amar to bid goodbye, Surama said, 'I'll be off now.'

'Right.'

'Have been rude to you many times. Forgive me if you can.'

She turned and was moving away when Amar hurried to her and held her hand. 'One moment please. Please admit only that. Please admit that you can still be a little sorry for me. We were a couple once, though we are not now. I had the licence to lay open my heart to you. With the right that I once had, I tell you what I hanker for. I just want you to think kindly of me, sometimes. I promise I will make no attempt to meet you ever again. Just admit that I am still a part of your life.'

Surama looked at her husband with wide, steady eyes and announced emphatically, 'I won't.'

Looking calm, she entered the large sedan waiting for her. Soon the various wings of the large mansion and its compound wall disappeared from view as if by magic.

She couldn't sit upright any longer and collapsed onto the car seat, weeping. 'I admit it. I admit it. You had the right to tell me how you felt once, and you still do. Yes, you are still a part of my life,' she said.

PART II

Chapter 1

The village of Kaligunj was situated where its feet were washed by the gently flowing waters of River Bhagirathi. Zamindar Radhakishore's sprawling residence overlooked the river. A beautiful garden was unfurled in front of the building, and its white gate was mounted by two gilded lions baring their teeth and showing their tongues in an unsuccessful attempt at scaring away passers-by. The white walls of the great house were bathed in the red-orange light of the setting sun.

On the second storey of the mansion, in a well-arranged room, the graceful figure of a lady could be seen at the window, working on her embroidery. With *zari* thread, she was stitching in motifs of flowers on a piece of velvet. That figure was none other than Surama's. Her long, loose hair spread carelessly over her shoulders and back, combined with a plain sari tinged with the colour of dusk, gave her an ascetic look. Surama was deeply involved in her work, oblivious to her surroundings, when a girl came into the room and demanded her attention. 'Ma, when are you going to be done with your work?' she asked. Though expressing displeasure, her voice had a natural charm. Surama smiled without looking up. The girl took hold of Surama's work and gave it a pull.

'Oh dear,' Surama exclaimed, 'that will spoil my flower!'

'What of that?'

'What of that? I have stitched it with such care. How can you spoil things so easily?'

'Why not? See, how easily I can undo the rose I had knitted so patiently.'

Surama looked at the girl with tender amusement. As she noticed the joyful smile on her fair, innocent face, she gave an involuntary sigh.

'What happened? Why did you breathe so deeply?'

'Nothing.'

'Something must have happened. Tell me, what it is.'

'Okay. So, you have no qualms about spoiling a woollen rose.'

'No.'

'But, how about a real rose? Would you be fine with tearing its petals, too?'

'A beautiful rose? As beautiful as the ones we have in our garden? I can pluck a rose and tear it, too, but it will be a pity. I will feel bad about it.'

Surama murmured to herself, 'Is the Almighty more hard-hearted than us?'

'What did you say?'

'Nothing,' said Surama as she tried to concentrate on her needlework. The girl cried out, 'Don't. Oh no! Don't start all over again, my dear Aunt!'

'Uma!' rebuked Surama.

'Sorry, sorry, sorry, Ma. I forgot for a moment. You are my mother now. Not just an aunt. Ma, please stop your work,' insisted Uma, the daughter of Surama's stepsister.

Surama gathered her work-things and put them carefully in a case. 'Go on, what do you want to tell me?' she asked.

'Nothing really,' said Uma. 'I was just wondering how you manage to work for so long at a stretch. Do you enjoy that?'

'Of course, I do.'

'I don't believe you do. How can a person be happy without speaking to anyone for so long?'

Surama pulled her visitor close to her. Parting the kid's loose hair with her fingers, she said, 'Is everybody a madcap like you to want to talk non-stop, in a high-pitched voice, with anybody who is near her? You see, some people like to converse with themselves. When they are conversing thus, they need to do something with their hands to prevent others from calling them mad.'

'When such people talk without anybody listening, whom do they actually speak to?'

'They speak to their own minds.'

'I don't believe such a thing is possible. I believe one needs someone else to talk to just the way Prakash and I talk to each other. Just the way I was speaking to him a while ago.'

'Had Prakash come to this side of the house?'

'Yes, he had. We were chatting for a long time. We waited for you to join us, but you did not come. So, he went away.'

'What were you two chatting about?'

'Oh, about this and that.'

'Okay, Uma. But why do you call Prakash only "Prakash"?'

'What else should I call him?'

'Prakash Dada or Prakash Babu.'

'Nobody had asked me to do that. Grandma called him Prakash so I do the same.'

'My *chhotoma*[12] called him only Prakash because he was a distantly related younger brother-in-law to her.'

'And I know that he is a distantly related uncle to you. Why don't you call him Uncle, then?'

'He is almost my own age. We had played together as kids, although we ended up living in different places afterwards. I would feel odd if I suddenly started calling him "Uncle".'

'And you expect me to not feel embarrassed if I suddenly started calling him "Dada" or "Babu"?' said Uma in amusement.

'But you have come to live in this house only about two years ago.'

'That's right. I came here after my mother's death. As soon as she died, Grandma brought me here.'

'And when did you come to your parents' place from your in-laws'?'

Uma's eyes widened as if she remembered something very striking. She let out a laugh to push away the bitter scenes that came to her mind. 'I came to my parents from my in-laws' place after that major incident in my life: my widowhood,' she said.

Surama suppressed a sigh.

'May I ask you something?' said Uma.

'Yes.'

'No, let it be. I am scared of being scolded by you.'

'I won't scold you. Promise. Ask me anything.'

'I just wanted to know why you all get so upset because

---

[12] The term 'chhotoma' means the younger mother in the context of the novel. It refers to Surama's stepmother.

I am a widow. Look how sad the word made you. Grandma, too, used to be sad whenever she remembered my condition. And my mother just wept and wept over it until all that weeping killed her.' The girl's beautiful eyes filled with tears as she expressed her dismay. 'Why, Ma? What is so sad about it? It doesn't make me sad. The word "widowhood" doesn't disturb me at all.'

Tears began to roll down Uma's cheeks. Surama tried to wipe them away with the corner of her sari. The teenager responded by hugging Surama and pressing her face to the older woman's breast. 'Ma, don't cry over what has happened to me. I think it is not all that bad.'

What could Surama say? How could she explain to the little one how devastating being a widow was for a woman?

Clearing her voice, she changed the subject. 'Uma, get me your comb. I want to tie up your hair.'

As it was the twilight hour and it was getting darker every moment, a maid came in and placed a lamp in the room.

'But it is already dark. You can't tie my hair now,' said the girl.

'I can. I don't mind whether it is dark or not.'

'But Haridashi says a widow should never tie her hair or wear any jewellery. Are all those rules really set for widows?'

'Maybe. But the rules are meant only for older widows, not for small ones like you. You were only eight when your husband died. Isn't it?'

'But now I am fourteen.'

'I know. Now, don't try to find excuses. Go and get your comb. Let me do your hair. Your grandma wanted you to always look well. Let us respect her wishes and keep you looking good, whatever may be the rules.'

When her hair was done, Uma said, 'You know, Ma, Prakash has brought me a beautiful bunch of flowers. Wait, I'll get it from the other room.'

Noticing the accidental similarities between the simple activities around her and the life she had left behind, Surama's thoughts drifted to the past, making her absent-minded. So, when Uma came back with her flowers and called 'Ma', Surama was startled. 'What happened? Why do you look surprised?' asked Uma.

'Oh, nothing much. When you called me, for a split second, I thought it was someone else's voice. You sounded exactly like Atul.'

'Atul, your son? But you know what Haridashi says? She says that Atul is not your own son.'

'He is my son. I have asked my relatives to bring him up.'

'What relatives?'

'My sister and her husband.'

'So, it was just like Haridashi to tell me all that rubbish…'

Surama looked at Uma, about to speak—perhaps to explain to her the exact nature of her relationship with Atul. But then, she said nothing.

Taking out a large rose from her bunch of flowers, Uma said, 'Ma, will you put this in my hair?'

'Such a beautiful flower! Where did you get it from?'

'As I said, Prakash brought some flowers for me. He asked me to wear this one in my hair.'

'Why did Prakash give you flowers today? Did he say something?'

'Yes. He asked me to wear this rose in my hair.'

Surama looked lost for a moment; her face was clouded

with worry. The rose dropped from her hand. Uma picked it up. 'Ma, put it in my hair, please.'

Surama stood up. 'A widow should not wear flowers in her hair,' she said. Uma was stunned and sorry. 'Should I put it in a vase, then?' she asked.

'No, destroy it or just throw it out of the window.'

'Waste it? Why?' asked the girl, innocently.

'Just do it. I know you can trash a flower. You have told me so.'

'I can. But it would be a pity.'

'So be it.'

'Let me throw it out, then. Somebody else can pick it up,' said Uma as she dropped the flower below. Surama watched her, broken-hearted.

'And what will I tell Prakash when he asks me if I had worn that rose?' asked Uma.

'Tell him you have thrown it away as widows are not supposed to wear flowers.' It deeply pained Surama to utter those words, but she did not relent.

'Okay,' said Uma as she moved towards the door.

'Where are you off to?'

'To find a place to cry for my mother. I miss her.'

Surama came forward and hugged the girl. 'I am your mother now.' Then, she made her lie down. 'Put your head on my lap and relax,' she said.

The teenager remained quiet for a little while, using her new mother's lap as a pillow, but as soon as the tears at the corners of her eyes dried up, she smiled. 'I would love to meet Atul,' she said.

'Of course, you would. Let him grow up a little. I'll bring him here.'

At this moment, Zamindar Radhakishore entered the room calling Surama's name. Surama got up hurriedly. 'What Baba?'

'Just came to see what the two of you were doing this evening.'

'This madcap has kept me busy. We find so many things to chat about!' said Surama.

'Madcap…' smiled Radhakishore, amused. 'Yes, that's what she is. And I am sure she won't let you feel lonely, here.'

'I don't feel lonely at all. This girl keeps me happily occupied.'

Uma sat up and objected, 'She is wrong. She hardly speaks to me. She is always with her needlework.'

Both Surama and her father laughed.

Then the zamindar looked at his daughter's slim figure and was grave. 'Child, how thin you have become! Is this place not suiting you well?' he said.

Surama did not know how to answer him. Her father continued, 'Child, you are my only support now. And you, too, have no one else but me to look after you. Don't hesitate to tell me what troubles you.'

'Why, Baba? What can trouble me here—under your care, in my own home? Don't worry about me, Baba.'

'Then, why are you losing weight? Your hair is always uncombed and you never wear a good sari. It is almost six months since I brought you to live with me, but I have never seen you dress well.'

'Baba, it hurts me when you speak that way. Actually, I was never used to finery. Where I had been until now, there was no scope for me to wear fine clothes. So, I am quite unused to them.'

'I understand,' said Radhakishore with a sigh. 'It was my destiny. Anyway, try to forget the past. I am going for my evening prayers, now. But before I go, here is a small request. I want to see you taking better care of yourself. Old people like me have a bad habit of drawing comfort from things appearing right. But, looking at you the way you are, I feel troubled. I begin to worry.'

Radhakishore left the room. Surama sat in silence, eyes lowered as she contemplated. Uma said, 'Ma, let me tie up your hair. I would love to do that.'

'No.'

'Why?'

'How can I groom myself when my daughter cannot do so? She cannot even put a flower in her hair.'

Uma reflected for a while. Then she said, 'But the day you came here from your other house, you were looking like an ascetic—your hair uncombed just like it is now—though you had not adopted me as a daughter yet. How come?'

'Don't you see how old I am? I have outgrown my days of dressing up.'

'Of course, not. I know what is wrong with you.'

'What?'

'You miss them. And you feel bad that you have left them behind to miss you—to cry for you. You feel bad because you have left Atul back there without his mother to love him.'

Surama covered her face. 'Oh Uma, stop it! Don't torture me by reminding me of them.'

Chapter 2

Surama had been living with her father for about six months now. Anyone else would have taken some time to adjust to the routine of a place she hadn't been to for several years, especially after living an altogether different life. But that was not the case with Surama. She could adapt to any change that came into her life. Things that had never happened before, nor had given any indication of happening ever, were faced by Surama with the same calmness that she showed while handling everyday affairs. She was prepared to deal with whatever life threw at her—conscious of the fact that she would hate herself if she failed to do that.

Despite her adaptability, things were not so simple. If she had come to live in her childhood home two years ago, she would have embraced it as her haven for the rest of her life. But the state in which she had left her marital home to come to her father's, filled her mind with guilt. She had no regrets about showering Charu with sisterly affection over the years, nor did she regret treating Atul as if he were her own son. But why did *they* love her so much? Why did she make *that* happen? Who were they? What did people call them? For people, Surama and Charu were co-wives, and Atul was the son of a supposed rival. Yet, Charu and Atul had given their hearts to Surama without a trace of inhibition. And Surama herself? Shame on her! That she loved them was a laughable matter—perhaps the wittiest joke in the world.

Did Surama think of Amar, too? Yes, she did. She perceived him as a curse—an ill-fated planet determined to ruin her life and steal every joy from her. She had now hardened her heart against the offer of love he had made in the recent past. She was convinced that his amorous sentiments for her were only a passing weakness, which had either already run its course or would do so soon. Unfortunately, it was *her* life that was permanently twisted by it.

Surama was greatly troubled by the way she herself had started feeling for him. It was a delusion, she was sure. So, she tried to shove into the depths of her consciousness what she thought was petty and shameful. Her heart wanted to love whom? A man who was married to another woman? Fie on her! What could be more degrading than loving a man who deserved the harshest of sanctions from her? Just after leave-taking in Manikgunj, Surama was overpowered by a sudden, strange longing for Amar, though it was only for a short period. Later on, she reflected that it was probably a temporary feeling stirred by the last glimpses of a place and people she had grown accustomed to over the years. Surama did not blame herself for feeling the pangs of separation so deeply at that time. In her mind, she rebuked Amar for pressurizing her to show affection for him. If he, the man, could act so irresponsibly, then she, the woman, might be excused for her temporary weakness.

After the conversation with her father that evening, Surama realized that he took her indifference towards clothes as a sign of missing Manikgunj. She was embarrassed. It was a pity, she thought, that people judged women and their feelings by what they wore and how they styled their hair—as if wearing jewellery and combing their hair attractively were among their important duties. Why did the Almighty create such wretched beings—beings who had to be guided by other people's opinions on even the garments they chose for themselves?

She was by nature indifferent to her looks. She took no interest in making herself attractive to others. But saddened by her father's remarks she, at once, picked up a comb and thoroughly brushed her hair, styling it into a beautiful coiffure. Then, she draped herself in a well-laundered sari.

It had not taken Surama much time to become a sincere well-wisher of Uma. She thought about her a lot. She knew that the world would never look kindly upon Uma and Prakash having any degree of personal interest in each other, and yet she suspected that some subtle power, transcendental in nature, was surreptitiously at work to bring them together. It was obvious that Prakash was besotted with Uma and his frequent company was likely to kindle a similar sentiment in her heart for him. But alas, any union of the two must only be a disaster as Uma was a widow. Something had to be done, thought Surama, before their gentle bond, as delicate, perhaps, as a string of flowers, turned into an iron shackle painfully tying them together. The best thing would be to keep the two young people apart.

Prakash was an orphan, the child of a distantly related uncle of Radhakishore. Slightly older than Radhakishore's own daughter, Prakash merged into his family like Surama's brother and was treated as such. Then, two years ago, Uma had joined his family. Indeed, Radhakishore had willingly accepted Uma's full responsibility, knowing that she had nowhere else to go. He was sure that when Surama came to live with him, she would lavish the young widow, unfamiliar with the ways of the world, with love and protect her from harm.

Considering how Uma and Prakash felt for each other, Surama thought it would be sensible to send Prakash elsewhere.

In her marital home, especially while her father-in-law was alive, Surama was an important adviser on business matters. That experience had recommended her to be her father's assistant, too, in the affairs of his estate.

One day while discussing business with the zamindar, Surama found an opportunity to broach the subject of Prakash's future. She drew his attention to how Prakash needed to visit the various sectors of their landholdings to gain knowledge of specific regional problems. Radhakishore was impressed and at once agreed to adopt the strategy. He immediately decided to post Prakash at Taherpur, for a certain period, to sort out some difficulties that had cropped up there.

It was well known that Radhakishore wanted to go on a long pilgrimage and was expecting Prakash to take charge of his zamindari during his absence. That was the reason Prakash was called home from his university as soon as he had completed his entrance course. Radhakishore had never hired a manager or a steward, viewing them as a nuisance. He, however, was ready to delegate responsibilities to Prakash as he was part of the family.

Soon, the day came for Prakash to leave for Taherpur.

Surama took care to prevent Prakash and Uma from meeting privately that day. She feared that the parting words of Uma's admirer, if meant only for her ears, might give rise to unwanted feelings in the girl's heart.

Coming to take his leave from Surama, Prakash found Uma with her, absorbed in learning to make *shondesh*.[13] The end of her sari tied around her waist like a belt and her hair pinned in a top knot, Uma was doubtlessly enjoying every moment of the experience. The sound of sweets sizzling in a pan and the clatter of cooking tools filled the place with a joyous vibe. Surama had chosen a lighter task for herself. She was only announcing the steps of the recipe as she kneaded some dough.

Looking handsome in his travelling clothes, Prakash stood at the door of the kitchen. He looked sad. Obviously, the prospect of leaving Kaligunj did not fill him with joy.

'Come in, Prakash,' said Surama.

'Hi, Prakash,' said Uma, stopping her work for a moment. 'All dressed up? Where are you off to? Oh, I remember—to Taherpur. So, are you leaving today?'

'Yes, today,' said Surama, 'and just now. Bring a plate, Uma. Serve some shondesh to Prakash.'

'Not now,' said Prakash. 'Just had lunch. Have taken a *paan*[14] too.'

'Come on, it doesn't matter. Taste some shondesh. And, Uma, be careful with those sweets. The ones in the pan are almost burnt!'

Ashamed, Uma turned to attend to the pan. Prakash came into the kitchen and sat down. He picked up a sweet

---

[13] A type of sweetmeat

[14] 'Paan' is a preparation made from betel leaves. It is commonly chewed after meals.

from the plate kept before him. 'This is enough for now,' he said while eating it.

'Don't you like it?' asked Uma.

'I like it, but it is not the right time to have shondesh.'

'Indeed, it is!' said Uma, playfully. 'Because you won't be here to have them later.' She looked at Prakash with clear, innocent eyes that radiated a fun-loving spirit.

Prakash stared at her, feeling a little surprised and also a little hurt. He was not expecting this. He was expecting at least a doleful look from Uma—a look indicating that she would miss him when he was away. Lost in thought, he ate up all the shondesh on his plate. After washing his hands, he said, 'It's getting late. I must get going now.'

'Don't say "going",'[15] reminded Surama.

Prakash smiled—a smile saturated with pain. 'Will be coming back, Surama, Uma.'

Uma nodded.

'Whenever you get the time, write to Baba,' said Surama.

Prakash agreed and left.

Surama, too, was sad. 'I regret being so cruel but, in this case, there was no choice,' she said in her mind. It was not in Surama's nature to tolerate what she thought was wrong. She would go to any lengths to check it. And she thought it was wrong of Prakash, however tenderly he did it, to try to rouse Uma's feelings for him, given the circumstances.

To divert Uma's mind, Surama said, 'Arrange the best sweetmeats on this plate. Let us send for Baba. Let him taste some of these, too.'

---

[15]In Bengal, it is customary to use the phrase 'will come back' instead of saying 'going'. This is part of the traditional leave-taking practice.

While doing as she was told, Uma asked, 'Ma, when will Prakash come back?'

'Can't say. You know, the experience of working in Taherpur will give him an opportunity to learn. That will be good for his career. Ultimately, he must look after a large zamindari. Knowing the ropes would help him.'

'I see,' said Uma. Then, after a while, she asked again, 'He might have to stay there for a month or two, perhaps?'

'Could be. Look, Baba is coming. Let us prepare a seat for him. You start frying the sweets that are left.'

Uma sat again on a low stool with a spatula in hand. She concentrated on gauging the temperature of the cooking medium on the stove and examining the shapes of the raw sweets for any defects.

When Radhakishore Babu, after tasting the sweets, said, 'Uma, they are delicious! You have become an expert at making shondesh,' Uma was overjoyed. She, however, felt a twinge of guilt for taking all the credit. She said, 'But, Ma has helped me a bit.'

'That was nothing. I did very little,' Surama protested. 'You really have talent. And over there, in that other place, Charu would not get it right even if I made her do this two hundred times.'

'Charu, your sister? Is she worse than me in this?'

Surama felt a little awkward after she inadvertently took Charu's name in her father's presence. 'This last batch of the sweets will be the best, I think,' she said trying to change the subject. 'Remember to dip them gently in the syrup.'

Radhakishore wiped his mouth after enjoying his treat. 'Prakash is a dependable and obedient boy,' he said. He wanted to share his good opinion of Prakash with Surama.

'He was ready to go to Taherpur as soon as I asked him to, though I know he did not like the idea of being posted there. Prakash has the qualities of a good manager. I am sure he will be successful in life.'

Complimenting Uma, again, on her culinary skills and showering blessings on her, the zamindar proceeded to attend to his other duties.

Uma arranged the sweetmeats on a large tray, intending to distribute them among all the members of the household. She left the kitchen, eagerly anticipating praise for her efforts.

Alone in the room, Surama's heart went out to Prakash. She imagined him on his boat to Taherpur—a sad and lonely figure—and wondered whether God had created her for the very purpose of breaking hearts and crushing the sprouting of innocent love in them. She shivered at her cruelty.

Uma derived great pleasure from listening to stories about Charu's inefficiency. When telling such stories to Uma, Surama's tone would betray her affection for Charu. Uma would complain, 'You are being partial, Ma. You love someone even though she is clumsy and forgetful, while you never praise me enough even though I am neat and careful in whatever I do.' Amused, Surama would laugh and say, 'That is because you are the naughtiest of all the people I love!'

Chapter 3

'Just to inform you, Uma,' began Surama, coming to where the adolescent was busily making sandalwood paste.

'What?' asked Uma, looking up from her work. With waves of loose hair adorning her face and shoulders, and a spotless white sari enveloping her slender form, she looked like a handful of *shefali* flowers ready to be offered to God. On a throne in front of them sat an idol, surrounded by the items needed for his worship. Surama looked at Uma, whose face, she thought, was as serene as one of the puja flowers. 'You are not allowed to have desires,' she said in her mind. 'So, I offer you to God. Let Him keep you away from longings, temptations and worldly crudity. I must occupy myself with instructing you on how to transcend earthly desires. And, in my attempt to do so, if I need to be harsh with you sometimes, God will forgive me that cruelty.'

The way Surama was looking at her made Uma laugh. 'Why are you staring at me like that, Ma? And, what did you come to tell me?' she asked.

'Just that...that Prakash has come back.'

'Really? When?'

'Sometime in the night.'

'Have you met him?'

'Not yet. But I've sent for him.' Surama turned as if about to go away.

'Ma,' said Uma. 'I cannot leave this room because the *purohit*[16] will arrive anytime now. Can't Prakash come here?'

'Yes, he can. In fact, I have asked him to come here and see us both.'

Uma started rubbing the stick of sandalwood on its stone tablet with joyful vigour. She looked up with a smile. 'Don't expect me to touch his feet now that I am doing this work.'

By that time, Prakash had arrived at the hall in front of the puja room. 'Come, Prakash,' Surama welcomed him.

'I'm still in my travelling clothes. Can't enter the shrine.'

'Then, stay at the door.'

Removing his footwear, Prakash came and stood at the puja room door. As he quickly glanced into the flower-bedecked room, he was met by two happy, bright and excited eyes full of warmth for him. He had to avert his gaze to break their spell. Smiling, Surama said, 'Prakash, the deity is waiting for your homage.'

Embarrassed, Prakash offered his obeisance to the god.

'And how have you been, Prakash, for all these months?'

'Quite well. Thank you.'

'It is our time now to formally touch your feet as you have come after a long absence. But I am sure, with you, I won't be able to do that—not now and not ever.'

'And I can never accept any pronams from you,' said Prakash, smiling.

'But Uma cannot be spared,' said Surama. 'Come, bow to him.'

---

[16] A Hindu priest or a person who performs religious and spiritual rituals and ceremonies.

'But I am making sandalwood paste,' said Uma, shy and uneasy.

'Even so. I'll do the paste while you perform your pronam.'

Uma got up, self-conscious but smiling. She came and touched the ground before Prakash's feet with her forehead. As the contact made quite a sound, Surama exclaimed with concern, 'Bless you! Why so hard? Wanted to break your head or what? Mad girl. Is it hurting badly?'

Uma, subdued, rubbed her brow. 'No, no, it's not hurting.'

Prakash merely looked at her.

Surama looked at Prakash, 'She did such a huge pronam, but I didn't see you blessing her.'

'Sorry,' said Prakash. 'But I don't know how to bless. Teach me.'

Surama said solemnly, 'Tell her, "Be pure. Be as pure as a flower offered to God."' Prakash looked at Surama and blushed. What exactly was she trying to tell him? But he was in control of himself the next moment and said 'Be as pure as a flower offered to God' quite naturally. Uma touched his feet in return. The three of them chatted for a while before the young man left the hall.

'Why were you so tongue-tied today?' Surama asked Uma when Prakash was gone. 'You hardly spoke to him.'

'Just felt very shy,' replied Uma.

'Why?'

'It was awkward to be with him after so long.'

'I see. But I was meeting him after months, too. I was not shy.'

'Perhaps, because you are a grown-up,' said Uma, after a little thought.

'Silly girl,' remarked Surama. 'Speak normally to him

when you meet him next. However, now that you are coming of age, you should be careful about some things. Don't converse with a man when you are alone with him. You can chat with all of them in my presence, but not otherwise.'

'Okay,' said Uma. Then she raised her beautiful eyes and asked innocently, 'Suppose, by chance, I meet a man or even Prakash himself, and suppose he begins to talk to me. What do I do, then?'

'Answer him in monosyllables and leave the venue as quickly as possible.'

'Okay. I'll remember.'

'You know, Uma, it doesn't sound good if you call Prakash only by his name. Start calling him Prakash Dada. Now that you are meeting him after a long time, it won't be too difficult for you.'

Smiling shyly, Uma said, 'It'll sound so odd.'

'You'll get used to it soon.'

Happy days followed. Surama kept Uma busy with the activity the teenager cherished the most—making shondesh. Radhakishore and Prakash were regularly invited for tea-time snacks in her special kitchen. The zamindar was a serious culinary critic. So, Uma would be thrilled by his praise, and in her delight, would serve him more and more sweetmeats. Prakash ate his snacks quietly, appearing to concentrate deeply on his food. In between entertaining the zamindar, Uma remembered to attend to him, too, and asked him eagerly, 'Don't you like them, Prakash Dada?' Prakash would hurriedly answer, 'Of course, I do.' Then, Radhakishore would say, good-humouredly, 'No doubt, he likes them. Look at his plate. While I talk and waste time, he continues to eat. After he finishes, not even a tiny crumb will be left for the ants. At this rate, the poor ants will be starved.'

That would be a joke repeated frequently by Radhakishore, eliciting genuine laughter from young Uma. Amused at Uma's cheerfulness, Surama and Prakash would smile, too.

∞

One evening, Surama sat alone, reflecting. It was an unexpectedly humid hour. The sky was overcast, and there was no pleasant breeze. The leaves on the trees were motionless. The temperature had dipped suddenly, making people shiver a little from time to time. The weather indicated that autumn had proceeded towards winter. Uma had come to call her Ma, 'Come, Ma, time to prepare the *prasad*.'[17]

'You do it by yourself, Uma, please. I am a little tired today.' Uma left, but Prakash approached her on business just after a while. 'Surama, Dada wants to consult you on the administrative changes we are thinking of making in Taherpur. Come, he is waiting.'

'Prakash, I am not too well today. Will you ask Baba to excuse me for a few hours? I promise to join you both later in the evening.'

However, the young man did not go away at once.

Prakash was hardly older than Surama. They had been playmates in childhood. Surama's years in her marital home had created some distance between them, but their friendship had started to flourish again now that they were

---

[17]'Prasad' is a term used in Hinduism to refer to religious offerings that are given to devotees as a blessing or as a mark of gratitude. These religious offerings can include fruits, flowers, sweets and other food items that are offered to a deity during a puja or religious ceremony.

associates once more. They had come back to their teasing and leg-pulling terms. 'Are you indisposed physically or is it a matter of the heart?' he asked.

'Maybe both,' said Surama, smiling.

As Prakash left to meet the zamindar, he felt a little sad for Surama. He was aware of the misfortunes in Surama's married life and could guess, almost correctly, how she felt.

What was Surama thinking, sitting there, on that occasion? Perhaps even she did not know. She had developed some weird symptoms recently. From time to time, she became inattentive to her surroundings. Her work dropped from her hands. And she struggled to breathe. Her eyes were unfocussed. She seemed to be lost in her inner world, weighed down by some baffling heaviness inside her. Perhaps that evening, she was thinking, 'Was this the final destination after my extensive journey? A grey place where nothing was properly defined? A place devoid of the excitement of happiness and misery?'

Surama felt as if her life was a clump of algae, carried away by the waves of an ocean. Rootless, it had no connection with any object of the world and moved wherever the currents took it. What kind of life was that? Was that a divine curse? Was it not worse than being struck by doom? The life which left no scope for regret or no excuse for shedding tears was, perhaps, as insipid as death.

Ahalya had turned into a slab of stone by the curse of a *rishi* (sage).[18] Was someone's wrath turning Surama into stone, too? Her father's unbounded love for her, Uma's total submission to her will, and Prakash's genuine friendship—

---

[18]This refers to a mythological story from the Ramayana.

these were wonderful assets she possessed. Unfortunately, none of them was able to lift her spirits. For a few months after coming to Kaligunj, she had forced herself to remain constantly alert, teaching herself the manners she needed to have in the altered status of her life. Now that everything was running smoothly, she did not need to be extra careful. Dark boredom threatened to engulf her mind and body. It made her feel as if she was transforming into an inanimate object. Was there anybody anywhere who could rescue her from such an end and put life back into her?

A few days later, when it was evening, Uma was in front of their household shrine, busy cleaning and arranging the *aarti*[19] lamps to be used by the priest a little later. Hearing footsteps, she thought Surama had come. As Uma had something to tell her, she turned to look and uttered 'Ma…'. It was not Surama who had come, though. It was Prakash. Uma was a little surprised as Prakash never came to that area of the mansion in the evening. She asked with concern, 'Prakash Dada, what happened?'

'Nothing,' said Prakash a little awkwardly. 'But, where is Surama? I wanted to meet her.'

'She must be somewhere upstairs. Come, I'll help you find her.' As was her wont, she got up with alacrity and hurried towards the staircase.

Prakash looked at the departing figure as if he was in a trance. The moon in its eighth-day crescent—fleeced in soft, white clouds—was swiftly moving away in the sky. 'Stop, Uma,' Prakash called almost against his own will.

---

[19] 'Aarti' is a Hindu religious ritual that involves offering a lamp and various symbolic items such as flowers and incense to a deity or a sacred object.

Uma returned. Surama's advice of being cautious when she was alone with a man, flashed in her mind, once. But wonder and curiosity brought her back. Standing at a little distance from Prakash, she asked, 'What is it, Prakash Dada?'

Without saying anything, Prakash kept staring at her. Perhaps, he was thinking, 'Doesn't she understand? Isn't she a woman? Is she a strange flower whose beauty and fragrance can be appreciated only from afar?'

Prakash's stare made Uma nervous. But she was also genuinely concerned for him. She came a little closer and asked with real sympathy, 'Are you not well, Prakash Dada? Shall I go and call Ma?'

'Uma,' said Prakash with passion. 'Don't you realize how I feel? Show me that you care. Every day you mesmerize me with your gestures. Are those gestures only the spontaneous expressions of a child? Give me some hint that they are more than that.'

Uma was stunned. What tone of voice, what style of speech, was that? Though she didn't understand the meaning of every word Prakash spoke, some unspecified alarm and some sensation never felt before made her shiver.

Finding Uma silent, Prakash resumed, 'Uma, say something, please. I can't bear this uncertainty anymore! I am going to Taherpur for a long stay this time. In that lonely, friendless and monotonous outstation, can I know that somebody is waiting for my return? That somebody is missing me?'

Uma was trembling with genuine fear. Her eyes, fixed on Prakash, had tears in them.

Misunderstanding the tears as Uma's expression of reciprocal feelings, Prakash said, 'Don't cry, Uma. Sorry that I hurt you. Just tell me that you'll miss me when I am gone. That tiny bit of truth will sustain me through all the gloomy days in Taherpur. That'll be my only gift to take back from this place. Uma, just let me hear your voice.'

Uma turned and looked down. 'Go away,' she said.

'Yes, I'll go. God knows why I said all that to you today. I had not come prepared for this. But believe me, Uma, the memory of these few moments spent with you will give me great joy in Taherpur. I know that you will forgive me when you understand how precious this encounter with you was to me. Shall I leave you, then?'

Covering her face with her hands, Uma moaned, 'Go away, go away. Why did you tell me all that? Why did you come here to meet me?'

'I don't know. I don't know, Uma. I had no intention of speaking to you that way, but suddenly, as I looked at you this evening, the words poured out of me...'

'I don't want to listen to you anymore,' Uma screamed in panic.

'Goodbye, Uma.' Prakash thought to himself: 'Oh God, why did I do this? Punish me if You will, but make Uma happy.' Prakash turned and walked away quickly, but Uma collapsed on the ground like someone pierced by a hunter's arrow. She felt an acute pain inside her—a sensation totally new to her. 'My God, what is happening to me? Why am I feeling this way? Deliver me from this, God,' she prayed.

Many of us have seen how a wild bird, unaware of human habits, behaves when it is brought among people and forcibly put into a cage. Immensely agitated, the bird hits the bars of the cage repeatedly. Struggling to come out, it ignores the blood-smeared injuries it causes to its own body. If a human hand kindly approaches to caress it, the bird tries to bite it hard.

When a person who has spent her days floating on life's bittersweet events like a flotsam on a water body, suddenly dips deeper into it even for a short duration, her desperation to return to her former state is somewhat like a defiant, newly caged bird.

Issues that are responsible for one's happiness or misery may sometimes occur so early in life that one is unable to register their significance. Not having felt the sharpness of a tragedy when it actually happened, one is forever free from the grip of its pain. Such a one can lead a childlike life. Like a delicate flower, that one can spread only fragrance. Uma was such a person. She drew pleasure from simple occurrences and laughed easily. She cried easily when hurt, but minutes later forgot what had hurt her and laughed again. Others felt sorry for her status in life and sometimes shed tears for her. When her loved ones behaved this way, it amazed and amused Uma. Only occasionally, and only for a little while, did that make her reflect on her fate because she had no clear idea of what was wrong with her life.

All that tranquillity of mind suddenly vanished for Uma. Being ignorant of a dimension of womanhood, she was stunned at its abrupt revelation. She lay on the floor, perplexed and scared, when she felt Surama's hands lifting her head onto her lap and her gentle fingers running through her hair. Uma continued to sob for a while. Then she sat up and looked, not at Surama, but the other way. 'Come, let's go and watch the aarti,' said Surama.

By then the little decorative lamps—scores of them—were lit in the temple. The priest, his face rapt with devotion for the god in front of him, stood erect and dignified, his hand rhythmically moving the platter of aarti lights that Uma had kept ready for the occasion. Uma kneeled in front of the idol and bowed her head. This was her place. It was she who had made that idol beautiful by adorning it with her own hands. The tray which held the five lamps that she had oiled and wicked and arranged on it, was the five-mouthed messenger avowing her deference to the god. As she stared at the idol, a sense of both exhaustion and fascination washed over her.

That night, on the large bed that they shared, Surama, lying close to Uma, gently stroked her head. But Uma moved away and turned towards the opposite wall. Surama's affectionate caresses irritated her. After waiting for a long while, Surama asked, 'What has happened, Uma? Why were you crying downstairs? Did you suddenly remember something sad?'

Uma said, 'Nothing. Nothing happened to me.' However, those simple words of denial sounded like cries of agony.

'Why were you crying, then, Child? Did somebody say something to you?'

'I don't know. Don't ask me. Nothing happened,' cried Uma.

Surama pulled the girl nearer and hugged her gently. Tenderly, she said, 'Why are you behaving like this, Darling? You have never hidden anything from me. Please tell me what has happened today.'

'Nothing,' repeated Uma, struggling to free herself from Surama's loving embrace.

Surama did not ask her anything further. She loosened her grip on Uma but did not release her altogether.

In the morning, Surama found Uma lying at the edge of their bed, sprawled out like a bunch of lilies devastated by a strong wind. Surama could tell that the child was awake but pretending to be asleep. What could have transpired to distress her so much? Of course, Uma had the right to mourn her fate and be depressed from time to time. But that kind of sorrow was not likely to make her hide things so stubbornly. Earlier, Uma would cling to people when she was sad instead of trying to get away from them. Rather than rejecting Surama's embrace, Uma would use her lap as a comfortable pillow for herself. Surama had no doubt that something terrible had happened to Uma. But what? 'Time to get up, Uma,' she said softly. Uma sat up on the bed. 'Come, let's take a walk in the garden,' said Surama.

While watching Uma's face keenly, Surama asked, 'Do you know that Prakash went to Taherpur, again, last night?'

The mere mention of Prakash's name hit Uma like a bolt of lightning. She turned her face away as her body started swaying slightly. Surama's face darkened. After a few moments of reflection, to test her doubts, Surama asked, 'Why didn't you come to bid him farewell when he was leaving?'

Uma covered her face and cried, 'I don't want to meet him!' Then she slowly lay down on the bed, again, closing her eyes.

A while later, Surama called, 'Dear Uma, get up now and take a bath.' Uma got up and was about to go to the bathroom when a maid came in. 'Uma Didi, won't you go to the shrine? The priest is waiting for you.'

'Dai, Uma is not feeling well. Please request the priest to prepare for the puja himself this morning,' said Surama.

Chapter 4

One evening, as she was feeding their second child, the infant Khuki, in their mansion in Manikgunj, Charu remembered how well Surama looked after babies. 'What a wonderful person my didi is!' she exclaimed.

Amar, who was reading a paper nearby, said, 'How odd you are.'

'You mean, it is not proper for me to praise Didi?'

'That's right. Aren't you two co-wives? Who on earth has ever loved such a rival?'

'Unfortunately, she isn't that to me.'

'Really? Don't be so conceited. Don't think you are above the ordinary.'

'Conceit? No, it's not conceit. It is my guilty conscience that makes me feel that way. I have deprived her of her husband, her home, and her right to have a child. And now you won't even allow me to love her a little?'

Amar remained silent for a while. Such reasoning from a woman, whom he thought only childlike, surprised him. A certain kind of fervour was attempting to build inside of him, which he suppressed with an effort. 'You are wrong, Charu, when you count yourself as guilty,' he said. 'It is I who should be blamed for everything. No need for you to share my guilt.'

'It was for me that you had acted that way,' said Charu.

'Where would I be if you had not married me? But by doing so, you have offended God and have broken another woman's heart. Who, other than I, should repent?' She looked down to hide the tears that were welling up in her eyes.

Neither of them spoke for a while. Then, Amar said, 'What has happened has happened. Don't brood over it. And indeed, it's I, and not you, who should feel ashamed. It pains me to see you suffer for what I have done. I, however, want to warn you of something: the person for whom you feel so deeply, the person whom you think you have hurt, doesn't really care about your sentiments. It is possible that she was tormented by my actions at the very beginning of our relationship, but later, she chose to carve out her own path. Hasn't she deliberately moved away from our company? She doesn't yearn for your or our friendship anymore.'

'You are wrong, there,' said Charu with emphasis. 'Love doesn't work that way. It cannot be one-sided. When I love somebody, it is understood that that somebody wants my love, and cherishes my love. One cannot love people who do not respond to it. People like that are lifeless dolls. Didi is not one of them. However, I won't deny that she avoids connecting with you. I think it's her wounded pride that restricts her from doing so.'

'Wrong, wrong!' objected Amar, vehemently. 'She has no pain. There's only indifference between your didi and me. No feelings are involved.'

'Do you want me to believe that she is incapable of love? That she never loved you? I even feel that you, too, had loved her once.'

Amar did not reply. Some time passed in silence. Then he said, 'It's getting late. I've work pending in the nursing home. Two of our patients are under critical care.'

※

On his way to his nursing home-cum-guesthouse, Amar met Shyamacharan Roy. The diwan had some sheets of paper in his hand. 'Amar, have you finished your morning round? You need to read and sign these documents. They require your approval.'

'Uncle, I still need to visit some patients. I promise to come to you immediately after lunch to do those papers.'

The diwan went away to finish other work while Amar hurried towards the infirmary. Seeing him approaching, an attendant rushed to meet him. He said, 'Maharaj, a gentleman, well dressed but very ill, has come staggering here and has fallen on that charpoy near the gate. We can't make out what he is trying to say.'

'Oh my God!' exclaimed Amar. 'And how are the two other critical patients?'

'They seem to be stable now.'

'Then, let me examine the person who has just arrived.'

On the string cot, a man with a very high fever was tossing about. Amar felt his pulse, looked at his face, and uttered in astonishment, 'Why, I know this fellow!'

Indeed, the afflicted one was someone very close to Amar, though they had been out of touch for years. 'Deven, Deven, my brother,' said Amar, anxiously. 'Why are you here and in this state?' Amar's febrile visitor did not answer. After a few more attempts to find out his whereabouts, Amar gave up. Instructing his assistants to arrange for a palanquin and bearers to transport his friend to his own residence, he went to attend to the other patients in the nursing home. Finishing his work, there, as swiftly as possible, he lifted his friend and put him gently in the palanquin, himself, and walking with the bearers, took him home.

For the next four or five days, Amar hardly left Deven's bedside, treating him with utmost care. The patient responded well to the treatment, and in two weeks, was almost back to his normal self. Several weeks later, all traces of Deven's illness were gone.

It was now time for the two old friends to have some joyful hours together. As they walked together in the large garden of the mansion, exchanging their thoughts, they felt as if they had gone back to their student days. Sometimes, when Atul joined them, the three of them played games.

One day, while they were pleasantly occupied, Amar said, 'I cannot fathom, Deven, how on earth you managed to reach my infirmary as a sickly beggar. Who had asked you not to write to me about your intention of coming here?'

Devendra smiled a little. 'How could I write that to you when you had ignored so many of my earlier letters? After you left our village with Charu, no news of you came to me for several months. Then, of course, you wrote to tell me that you had married her. After that, you stopped replying to all my letters except for a few hurried words of acknowledgement to one or two of them. As you had decided to forget me, I, too, tried to forget you.'

'So, what additional misdeed did I do for you to remember me again?'

'Several of them, in fact. I was on a long tour of western India—in search of knowledge and peace of mind—and was sure that that sojourn would completely erase you from my memory. But on my return home, I heard that you had visited our village. I heard of your kindness to Tarini, that unfortunate cousin of Charu's, and was surprised to learn that you had even called on at my house and had enquired about me! Suddenly I was filled with a longing to see you.'

'Why did you come to the nursing home instead of my residence?'

'Just to have some fun. I had planned a big surprise for you. Finding me there was still a big surprise for you, of course, but the script went completely out of hand. Who would have known that the terrible Bengal Malaria would come creeping and pounce on me?'

'Anyway, now that you are here, I would be obliged if you spend some time with us.' Deven readily agreed with a big 'thank you'.

The two friends were walking beside each other as they conversed. Now, they continued to walk in silence. After a while, stopping in his tracks, Deven asked, 'Dear Amar, would you mind if I put a few questions to you? I'd dare to do that only if you tell me that I can be as free with you as I used to be earlier…'

Amused at Deven's solemn manner, Amar said, laughing, 'Skip the prologue and start singing your carol.'

'My questions are about your personal life. That's why I hesitate.'

'Carry on. I have nothing to hide from you.'

Deven paused for a second. Then, overcoming his embarrassment, said, 'Remember, how I had committed a blunder when you had neglected to inform me about your first marriage? I understand the reasons you had kept me in the dark about that wedding: firstly, because you felt a little ashamed to tell me that you had married a rich girl, and secondly, perhaps, because you were not exactly happy, yourself, with that marriage. Though it was only towards the end of her life that I had suggested to Charu's mother that you could marry her daughter, I had always believed that your principles would prevent you from marrying for wealth. Though you did not keep in touch with me even after your second marriage, I have a feeling that Charu has made you happy. Am I right or wrong?'

Amar did not reply immediately. A sea of memories, which had been stagnant in his mind for years, had suddenly begun to roil.

'Dear Deven,' he said after a while. 'I can hardly describe the predicament that led me to sever all connections with my friends and relatives. My father had disowned me. I had become destitute. It was a shameful life. In that state, how could I show my face to the people who knew me? Then, my father forgave me—whole-heartedly—after two years, but soon left this world himself. Life has been a roller-coaster ride ever since; the tumult has even shaken the basis of my own identity.'

Deven reflected for a while. Then he said, 'Perhaps it was my fault. Or maybe it was yours or maybe it was just your destiny. Whatever it was, its outcome was not good. A household with co-wives cannot be happy. One cannot expect the ladies to get along well.'

Amar blushed. Smiling, he said, 'That isn't the case, here, Deven.'

'Then, why do you seem to be fed up with life? I know Charu since she was a child. I can't imagine her hurting anybody's feelings. And I know that your first wife comes from a highly regarded family. So...'

'My first wife? She doesn't live with us. Charu is the only mistress in our house.'

Deven was surprised. 'Is that so? Where is your first wife, then?'

'In her natal home. She has been there for over a year now.'

'Before that, was she with you?'

'Yes.'

'Couldn't you settle things at home in all those years?'

Amar looked down and answered in the negative.

'I was mistaken about Charu, then,' said Deven. 'Charu is like my sister. I have a right to criticize her. I must say that she has not acted well here. She should have realized what was expected of her...'

'No, Deven. Charu is not at fault. If anybody is to be blamed, it is me.'

Deven's eyes widened. 'You misbehaved with your wife! Shame on you. Unfortunately, fate has also involved *me* in all this. So, she has left you hurt and neglected?'

Amar was quick to answer, 'No, no, no. It is not neglect but hatred.'

Deven reflected on that comment for a moment and then smiled. He said, 'Was it only hatred? Hatred for her husband doesn't come easily to a wife. Are you sure that something more complex was not at work? Fondness for you mingled with her sense of being deprived, for example?'

'Fondness for me? A husband who has no right to pride himself on being her husband?'

Devendra shook his head sadly. He said, 'The relationship between husband and wife is not written on water. It's a permanent mark sanctioned by God.'

'No point in analysing what it is. Suppose it is something that is written on stone. But, for it to be written neatly, one needs to be an able craftsman with fine tools. In case the stone tablet supposed to bear the message breaks into pieces at the very beginning of the project, I am sure that it can never be adequately repaired to be suitable for writing upon once again.'

'Let us find out if the tablet is really broken or not.'

'Spare me. At least for this lifetime. Help me pass the present one somehow or the other. Let us go for shikar tomorrow.'

Deven pretended to be surprised and said teasingly, 'Hunting? With the fat old man that you are now? Will you be able to carry a gun?'

'There is a slight chance that I may,' said Amar, joining in the joke.

Chapter 5

It was an especially severe winter. The woodland where Amarnath and Devendra went hunting was dark and cool, even in that mid-afternoon. Leafy trees like mango and jackfruit allowed only trickles of sunlight to filter through. The forest floor was, therefore, dotted with pale patches of light that looked like the weak smiles of people recovering from illness. One can surmise from the absence of any large species of resident birds that they had left their homes to sunbathe elsewhere. The jungle was unusually quiet. The only sounds that could be heard were the droning of cicadas or the screeching of old bamboo trees as they bent and stretched. Amarnath and his friend were the first human visitors in the forest after a long gap. Besides hunting equipment like guns and bullets, the two men had an ample supply of food and water. However, they had little success in finding any sizeable game to hunt. So, Amarnath urged his friend to kill some small birds.

'Brother, who would have the heart to kill those tiny things,' said Deven. 'In fact, this village of Bengal is quite unfit to provide one with a good hunting ground. During some of my visits to the western states of the country, I have seen great vultures. They would stare at me with twisted expressions—looks filled with hatred for the entire world. They scared me. They appeared as if one day they would become the most powerful biped on Earth. One felt as if killing them was one's duty. And here? Look at those gentle-looking birds on those clumps of bamboo. Look at those little waterbirds hopping about at the riverbank and around the ponds. One feels as if they need one's protection.'

Amar laughed. 'You were not so kind always. I remember you killing plenty of small birds on an afternoon eight or nine years ago…'

'Yes, I remember how I used to be. But that was before I had travelled much. After being in some dry and rocky terrains of this country, I fell in love with the greenery and wetness of my state. "Leafy mango groves", "pools shaded dark", "little peaceful villages in shade"—all have a hidden sweetness in them. I am truly ashamed of how I behaved that day, eight years ago. But, Brother, on that outing, you were, surely, the sharper hunter than me—what a big catch you had made!'

Amar smiled. 'Yes. How can I deny that?'

'It can be taken as proof that luck is always more successful than learning or manliness. Two of us had gone hunting. As a medical student who was senior to you, I could claim superiority in learning, and physically, I possessed greater manliness due to my size. Yet, luck was partial to you.'

'Don't blame your luck. I am sure the goddess of fortune wouldn't have frowned upon you if you had attempted to elevate your status from an elder brother to a more romantic figure in Charu's life.'

Devendra, in mock anger, levelled his gun at Amar's head as he said, 'How dare you suggest that!' Then, both friends burst into genuine laughter.

They reached the river. As it happened every winter, it

had dwindled into a narrow stream, creating a wide beach on either side. The sand particles glistened in the midday sun. At a distance, away from the river, fields of mustard, with their yellow flowers, looked like the golden aanchal of Goddess Lakshmi. Groups of small waterbirds took dips in the shallow bowls of water at the edges of the river, flew about in little circles, or just hopped about on the sand.

By and by, it was time for sunset. The mild sunbeams of winter playfully illumined the small waves of the river, before moving away to the sands of the riverbed, then further away to the tops of trees. From there, they continued to dissipate. As the western sky turned russet, the birds flew away to their homes. In the village on the other shore of the river, tired cows were making their way back home from grazing in the pastures. 'Let's go home now,' said Deven.

'Can't we spend the whole evening here and go home at night?'

'No. It's already late.'

Crossing the river in a dinghy, they walked home. When they arrived at Amar's mansion, darkness was deepening every minute. Rooms of the stately building gleamed with lamps. While Deven stayed behind to rest in the outer quarters of the house, Amar proceeded to the inner quarters.

Amar found Charu in bed. She had a high fever. She was shivering. Khuki, in her nanny's arms, was crying. Atul, not knowing what to do, ran from one room to another. He was relieved to find his baba back home.

Amar sat near his wife. 'Are you feeling very unwell, Charu? You are getting these episodes so frequently these days. It worries me...'

Charu's fever had gone in a few days, but Amar could

sense that she was not too well. Would a change of place for a few months help her to recover? He decided that it might. This time it was not difficult for him to convince Charu that a few months outside Bengal would be good for the whole family.

Chapter 6

Arrangements began for their tour of the western cities of India. Devendra was invited to join them. The family, now, had an additional member: Mandakini. She became one of their party, too.

Even Surama, in Kaligunj, through Charu's letters, was aware of who Mandakini was. In one of her letters to her didi, Charu had written:

Dear Didi,

You will be sad to know that Tarini Dada is no more.

Atul's baba had gone to see him on hearing that he was seriously ill. He was there with him for four or five days. On his deathbed, Dada begged Atul's baba to take charge of his only daughter, whose mother had died many years ago. (You see, our husband's fate seems to have a certain preference for such matters!) The girl is here. She must be about fifteen or sixteen. Tarini Dada had not taken any responsibility for her upbringing, and she was left with her mother's family until the last few months when Tarini Dada called her to be with him. By then, Tarini Dada had fallen critically ill and now he is dead.

Mandakini doesn't speak much and hardly smiles. Atul's baba says she is mourning for her dad, but I think she's quiet and serious by nature. I feel she is too wise for her age. Your Atul is very fond of her, though, and calls her 'Didi'.

Manda calls me 'Aunty'. When I was introduced to her as the mistress of the house, she touched my feet and stood quietly before me with her head bowed down, as if she were a beggar. The poor orphan.

Atul is well, as is Khuki. Atul often asks me why you live away from us now. I have to make up stories and tell lies to calm him down.

Yours only,
Charu

Before coming to Varanasi, the city they had chosen to spend a few months in, they visited Gaya, Allahabad, Agra, Vrindavan and Mathura.

As soon as they disembarked from their train in Varanasi, agents from various outfits—religious and secular—approached them, offering to provide guides and accommodation. Despite their incessant nagging, Devendra managed to rent a house of his choosing in a sunny and airy location close to Durga Mandir.

It was a bright morning after a few successive days of rain. At a distance from their residence, the row of buildings bordering the main city of Varanasi seemed to be smiling. Amar declared, 'This is the perfect day to watch morning aarti at Vishwanath's temple.'

As Khuki was slightly unwell, Charu had to reluctantly stay back. Amar and Deven went for what Charu and Amar termed their 'jatra'.

Not well aware of religious practices, Deven did not

know that visiting holy places was called jatra. So, hearing that they were going for a jatra, Deven asked, 'Do you mean to take me to a jatra show?'[20] Then, in his usual jocular manner, he announced that he was ready to perform in a regular play or even in a circus if Amar asked him to, but he would never act in a jatra set.

'No, no. This jatra is different, very auspicious,' Amar explained. 'Visiting temples of Varanasi is supposed to be as propitious as Ganga jatra.'[21]

'Thank Goodness!' said Deven with relief. 'I was even ready for Ganga jatra, lying in a cot, covered with a sheet, red flowers sprinkled on it, instead of watching a jatra charade. In my younger days, I went to watch a jatra once, called Ravan Badh. But as soon as I heard the bearded men, dressed like women, trying to portray tender-natured female characters, I ran. I ran as if I were a dog whose head was throbbing in pain after some poisonous insect had bitten it...'

'Okay. Enough. I have got your point. How you love to exaggerate things!'

'I speak the truth, however.'

Reaching the goddess's place, they heard that it was too early for Vishwanath's aarti to start. So, they decided to spend the interim period roaming around the menagerie kept in the compound of Devi's temple.[22]

---

[20]The term 'jatra'—which means a journey, especially to a holy place—also stands for a form of theatrical folk art of Bengal, quite crude in its presentation until its revival in recent decades.

[21]Some Hindus believe that the most dignified and spiritually advantageous form of dying is to touch the water of the Ganges while dying. Dying individuals are taken to the riverbank in order to achieve this spiritual goal.

[22]Annapurna Devi's temple is situated only fifteen metres north-west

Mischievously, for a while, they went about teasing the innocent creatures—scratching the cows' dewlaps, holding the peacocks by their long feathers, or catching the deer by their horns. Finally, Deven said, 'Enough of that. Behave yourself now, or Brother Nandi's golden staff will surely fall on your back.'[23]

'If that happens, it will only be because of my being in bad company—yours,' said Amar.

A group of people passing the menagerie suddenly started a ruckus, drawing the friends' attention. 'Can anyone tell me what's happening there?' Deven wondered aloud.

What they could make out was that an elderly gentleman with a prominent belly was caught among some especially troublesome *pandas*[24] as he was trudging towards Vishwanath's mandir. He must have been a rich man, judging by the number of people trying to fleece him and by the staff-wielding bodyguards he had with him, however useless they might have been in rescuing him. The crowd had grown in size as curious onlookers passing by had stopped to watch the commotion.

---

of the Kashi Vishwanath temple. Devotees usually pay their homage to Vishwanath before coming to bow to Annapurna.

[23] Deven is referring to a passage from *Kumar Sambhava*, one of the finest works of Kalidasa. In the third chapter of *Kumar Sambhava*, Shiva's gatekeeper Nandi, a golden staff in his left hand, the index finger of his right hand on his lips, is ordering the birds and beasts of Shiva's garden to keep quiet as their master is engaged in meditation. The mythical character, Nandi, is generally depicted as a bull, but he was born as a man. His face was transformed into a bull's face by a boon from Shiva to save him from a prediction of death at the age of eight.

[24] A class of priests who are often agents of other priests.

'Come, let's follow them and enjoy the fun,' said Deven.

'Of course not. Why give the touts a chance to pester us?'

'Actually, I really feel sorry for that old man. May I go and save him from his persecutors?'

'Don't. You will get into trouble yourself. Remember, the city of Varanasi is dominated by pandas of all kinds. By the way, I think I've seen that gentleman somewhere. Don't remember where, though.'

'No wonder. People of the same rank and status tend to keep meeting. Only, you still lack an aristocratic belly like his. You must work on that.'

'Enough of your gibberish. Now, let's hurry or we won't get a place to sit.'

'Seats will be available as long as you are ready to spend money from your pocket.'

Using that method, they found a place quite close to the idol of Vishwanath. The aarti had begun. Nine priests, each holding a lampstand fitted with multiple lamps, now alight and twinkling, showed their deep reverence for the god by moving their hands in unison in a rhythmic, circular movement. As they did so, they also chanted verses from Vedic hymns, their voices mingling with the beats of gongs, bells and cymbals sounded by groups of devotees standing near them. Burning incense sticks and camphor filled the venue with fragrant smoke. Two priests, each holding a large and beautiful whisk, stood on either side of Vishwanath, fanning him.

The charged atmosphere fascinated Amar as he looked around to take in the whole scene. Suddenly, his eyes fell on a known face in front of him. Startled, he looked away, his heart thumping for a few moments. The person who moved him that way was standing, raptly watching the aarti, where several other women had also gathered. So, while anxious to look again to check if he had identified her correctly, he had to be careful not to appear indecent. From where he was sitting, he could see the effigy of Vishwanath, too. By then, the deity was covered in flowers and bel leaves and the venue still echoed with the sounds of bells and other noises.

Amar managed to take another look. Yes, it was she—the woman he had known intimately for several years. Standing in front of the idol of Vishwanath, her hands joined and held on her chest in a gesture of supplication, her long, loose hair cascading down her back, a corner of her simple, raw silk sari hugging her neck in a half-circle—she looked like devotion personified.

Deven pushed him from behind. 'Amar, I can see that poor gentleman over there. It looks like two or three of the touts are still after him.'

Amar did not comment. But, by then, he knew who that gentleman was.

Deven said, 'Why don't we go and introduce ourselves and ask him if he needs any help? Then, we can share his bench, too.'

'No,' said Amar. 'Because I have remembered who he is.'

'What of that? I assure you he will not eat you up mistaking you as Vishwanath's prasad.'

'Who knows? And no need to socialize in such a strange place.'

'Amar, who is he?'

'Will tell you later.'

The aarti was going on. The crowd had pushed the friends very close together. Deven complained, 'This is an odd spot to be in. Whenever I lift my eyes, I see women. Those ladies are standing just opposite us.' Amar blushed. To divert Deven's attention from the subject, he said, 'Deven, why don't you go and meet that person, after all, and see if he can accommodate us on his bench.'

'If you do not have a problem, I will do that then.'

'I have no problem. Only, remember to speak respectfully with him.'

'Of course, I will.'

Deven moved away, making his way through the crowd.

Overcoming his embarrassment, Amar looked again towards that group of women, seeking one known face. The scene had not changed. A serenely patient figure was watching the aarti with all the attention of her heart and mind. She looked like an artist's creation in marble—a lady praying to her god.

By and by, the aarti was over. The time came for the devotees to bow to Vishwanath. For doing that, the lady, too, shifted her stance and her focus of vision, which, by chance, fell on another pair of eyes.

Amar looked away quickly. 'Deven,' he called. But of course, Deven was not standing behind him, then.

Deven was quite a few yards away. Pushing through the crowd, he was coming back to join his friend. As soon as his eyes met Amar's, he motioned him to come near. Amar remembered that he had still not paid his homage to Vishwanath. So, before stepping ahead to meet his friend, he turned and did his pronam. As soon as he did that, a long string of marigolds, thrown towards him by a panda wanting to thank him for his generous donation of money, encircled his neck. It amused Amar a bit, as the timing of that unexpected honour could be taken to mean that it was a message of blessing from Vishwanath himself. He moved a few steps backwards, took a good look at the god, and made another bow to him. There were quite a few ladies in that area, but all were unknown to him. Was that sudden vision he had had, a little while ago, a hallucination, then? But, no, the senior citizen sitting on a special bench a short distance away indicated that what he had seen was real.

When the friends were next to each other again, Deven said, 'That old gentleman is useless. He was not at all interested in getting acquainted with me. It seemed the lifestyles of the pandas and the beggars of Varanasi interested him more. You said you know him. Who could he be?'

'Do you really need to know that?'

'Was just a little curious.'

'He is a very honourable member of my extended family.'

'Is that so? Oh my God! How closely related is he to you?'

'Pretty closely. He is my father-in-law. I mean, people say that he is that to me.'

'Really? You should have told me before. Now, I've made such a bad impression on him.'

'I am telling you now. Stop teasing him.'

'Sorry. Shame on me...'

'It is all right. But now, let us run away from this place.'

'Could you see his wife among the women devotees here?'

'He's been a widower for many years.'

'I heard that his only daughter is his heir, too. Am I correct? Was she here today?'

'Yes.'

'You mean she is his heir or that she was here today?'

'I mean both.'

'What! That means you've seen her just now?'

Amar did not reply. The friends walked in silence for a while. Then, Deven spoke suddenly. 'I think you have not revealed the whole matter to me.'

'About what?'

'About your marital status, of course. You want me to believe that it is a common, family affair, but I suspect a hint of romance in it. I detect the material of a novel, here.'

Amar laughed. 'In the events of my life? No way. If anything, they can only add up to a humdrum farce.'

'Don't belittle Life. Life is a great adventure. It is either a tragedy or a comedy.'

'People who take life seriously are silly. It is just a farce.'

On reaching home, they found Khuki playing about. She had kept well after Amar and Deven had started for their jatra. Charu grumbled how she, being the mother, had to unnecessarily miss the trip to the temples. Amar consoled his wife by promising to take her there another day, soon.

After lunch, when Amar lay down for his siesta, Charu came to him for chit-chat. 'How was the aarti?' she asked.

'Nice.'

'People say the evening aarti is more beautiful.'

'Perhaps.'

'Will you take me to the evening aarti, then?'

'Yes.'

Getting irritated, Charu said, 'Why are you answering in monosyllables? What's happened to you?'

Amar realized it would be a mistake to conceal that morning's happenings from Charu. If she came to know about them from another source, she would wonder why her husband wanted to hide them from her. There could be repercussions.

Amar's voice trembled slightly as he said, 'Nothing much. I saw one or two known people in the temple today.'

'Who were they? Do I know them too?'

'Yes. Remember, you had been to Kaligunj once? I saw the zamindar of Kaligunj in the temple compound.'

'Didi's father? And you speak about it so casually? He's a highly respected relative of ours! Did he see you?'

'No.'

'Was Didi with him?'

'Maybe.'

'What do you mean by "maybe"? Could you see her?'

Amar cleared his throat and said, 'Yes, I did. I saw her.'

'Really? And you were not telling that to me? Was Uma Rani with them? And, Prakash Uncle? Was he there?'

'No, I did not see them.'

'They have not seen you, you say?'

'Right. They have not seen me.'

'We must meet. How do we let Didi know we are here?'

'We'll see.'

'Please, on my behalf, find a way to meet them.'

'I'll try.'

Two or three days passed. Amar went on finding excuses for not getting in touch with the Kaligunj people. He claimed that he had tried to obtain their address, but was unsuccessful.

Frustrated, Charu confided in her Deven Dada. After accusing her husband of sheer laziness, she convinced Deven of the urgency of finding Zamindar Radhakishore's address in Varanasi. That same evening, Devendra set out for the

Vishwanath temple to meet the resourceful panda who was responsible for providing a comfortable seat to the zamindar in the temple compound a few days back.

Chapter 7

Surama was quite preoccupied and looked distraught as she came out of Annapurna's temple and hurried to join her father in the courtyard. It was time to return home after their morning visits to holy places. She navigated her way through the crowd, guiding her father towards the exit. Uma followed them.

What had disturbed Surama was seemingly insignificant. At Annapurna's temple, she was unable to pray to the goddess. The thought that she had not worshipped Annapurna's husband Vishwanath before coming to worship Annapurna, made her uneasy.

They had been to Vishwanath's temple earlier. With her heart filled with devotion, Surama was holding up her flowers to put at the idol's feet when, suddenly, a man appeared between her and her god, giving her the impression that Vishwanath was refusing to accept her offering—as if the god was telling her to place her homage where it rightly belonged. And then, she had a glimpse of a well-known face.

She did not feel like making another attempt at bowing to Vishwanath that day, deciding that her gift for him had already gone stale. Those flowers, light and soft though they were, weighed like stones on her conscience. She wondered where she could throw them.

The *darshan*[25] of the gods and goddesses had given Radhakishore and Uma great satisfaction. It was nice to see Uma, who had been quiet and subdued for many weeks, exulting at the elegant enactment of the morning aarti in a temple. She said, 'How prettily the aarti was done, Ma! The atmosphere was suffused with a palpable sense of devotion. Everybody seemed to be participating in something uplifting. I felt as if the god had especially come there to bless his devotees after accepting their offerings. There was so much joy in bowing to a god in that place.'

Only Surama felt unblessed, the hollowness in her piety rebuked by Vishwanath.

The family had reached Varanasi some hours back and were yet to settle down in their accommodation there.

Making their temporary home ready for living was tiring work, even though Prakash had come with them to help out. In the evening when Surama was still setting up the place, Uma came to her with a message from Radhakishore. 'Ma, Dadababu (grandfather) would love to visit the Kedar Temple with us. Let's get ready.'

'No, Uma, we will go there tomorrow. Tell him we are too tired today.'

After some time, when Surama had come out of one room and entered another, she found Prakash looking out of a half-open window, an absorbed and mesmerized expression on his face. She tiptoed closer to look out, too, and found Uma on a veranda, totally unaware that she was

---

[25]'Darshan' refers to the act of seeing and being seen by a religious deity or guru, especially in Hinduism or Jainism. It is often used to describe a devotee's visit to a temple or shrine to receive blessings from the deity or guru.

being watched. Uma was busy polishing some small copper vessels that Radhakishore needed for his daily puja. Surama could not fail to read a subtly spiritual quality in Prakash's stare, which she could not but respect despite knowing that that was not something to be encouraged or admired. She came out of the room quietly, without disturbing Prakash.

The next two days were spent visiting several other holy places. As planned, Prakash was to leave for Kaligunj the next day. 'Dear Surama, can we spare Prakash?' the zamindar asked. 'Won't we request him to be here for a few more days?'

'No, Baba, let him go. Someone has to be there to look after things. We can manage here.'

'Okay, then,' said the father, reluctantly.

It was the zamindar's idea to call Prakash from Taherpur to accompany the family to Varanasi. Though Surama was opposed to this, she had agreed to let Prakash join them for a few days, to honour her father's feelings. Radhakishore had expected that Surama would not object to Prakash staying on after seeing how helpful his presence was in Varanasi. But Surama was too stubborn to allow that.

Surama was getting a basket ready with local fruits for Prakash to take with him. She called Prakash to give him instructions on how to distribute the fruits among the people back home.

'But, Surama, I suppose I won't be able to go today. The earliest I can leave is the day after tomorrow.'

'And, why is that?'

'I'll tell you why. Amar Babu has a friend by the name of Devendra. Do you know him?'

'Maybe.'

'He had come to meet me a while ago and has left a message for you, which says that Amar Babu, Atul and his mother are in Varanasi. He gave me their address and urged me to take you to meet them tomorrow.'

'Prakash, you don't have to stay back for that. You need to go home. Get ready for your journey.'

'Okay, if I must. But make sure to visit them tomorrow. They did not come here themselves as Dada might get annoyed if they did. But you must go.'

'I'll see.'

'Does that mean you won't go?'

'If they have reasons not to come here, I might have reasons not to go there.'

'But they are your marital family.'

'Whatever. But you cannot change your plans, Prakash. Your journey for Kaligunj is scheduled for today.'

'If you insist. But honestly, I was looking forward to meeting Amar Babu again.'

'That doesn't matter. But Prakash, I have a really serious subject to discuss with you.'

'Really serious? Be quick. Remember, you have asked me to leave this place as swiftly as possible.'

'It's not a joke, Prakash. Tell me, aren't you very keen to stay on here?'

'Of course, I am. Who wouldn't in such a pleasant and comfortable place?'

'Is that the only reason, Prakash? Look into my eyes and tell me if that is the only reason.'

Prakash shivered a little as Surama's bright, penetrating eyes looked into his. In a faint voice, he asked, 'What other reason can there be?'

'I know what is holding you here. Prakash, you have sinned. I am going to judge you and pronounce my verdict.'

The young man felt as if the ground was shifting under his feet. His ears buzzed. Stunned, he remained silent. Surama continued, 'Shall I disclose what mischief you have done? You have injected poison into an innocent girl's mind. A child widow, with a pristine heart, who is expected to remain that way her entire life, is suffering because you have tried to plant desire in her. Yes, you have sinned, Prakash.'

There was a chair nearby. Prakash sat on it. 'Sin?' he whispered.

'What else? You have tried to tempt her. You have revealed to her that she attracts you. She is a child widow, forbidden to receive the love of a living man, and yet you have communicated to her that you love her. In her early teens, she naturally craves love. Yet, she is too young and too simple by nature to recognize her vulnerability. But I am sure you are aware of the consequences, Prakash. Are you not ashamed of yourself?'

'Stop it, Surama. Have mercy on me...' pleaded Prakash.

'It might pain you to hear all this. But you are a man of the world—intelligent, educated, and much older than her. Imagine how she will suffer if she falls for you. Imagine the burden on her conscience when she gets convinced of her guilt...'

'No harm will come to her,' Prakash was quick to put in. 'She is untarnished. It's all my fault.'

'Good. Let's hope she is unaffected. May God protect her. But what will be your atonement for the sin you have committed?'

'Surama, I'll do whatever you ask me to do.'

'Are you sure?'

'Yes.'

'Remember, God is our witness.'

'Yes, He is.'

'Then, get married. Get married as soon as possible. Learn to love another girl. Let Uma never know that you had once loved her or that you continue to love her.'

Prakash could not say anything immediately. Dry-mouthed, he remained speechless.

'Prakash, have you heard me? Are you ready for your atonement?'

'I have heard you. You are a woman. How can you be so cruel? Suggest something else.'

'I can't. Getting married is the only punishment for you. If you can't accept that, run away. Run far away from us.'

'Won't you give me some time to think?'

'No. Uma must shed the false impression from her mind as quickly as possible.'

Neither spoke for a minute.

'If there's no option, I am ready,' Prakash announced abruptly. 'I'll do as you say. Am I going to be married today?'

'No. But soon.'

Chapter 8

It was almost noon. Her morning puja done, Uma came and stood on the veranda. She needed to dry her hair. Surama would scold her if she did not. In one hand she was holding some flowers and a wreath brought out from the puja room. She lifted her other hand to give a shake to the wet parts of her tresses, but, midway, forgot what she was going to do.

Surama gave her no option to brood, keeping her active throughout the day. But, whenever she found herself idle and alone, even if only for a few minutes, she would get lost in thoughts. The floral wreath held in her hand had suddenly reminded her of the incidents of a fateful evening. She was stringing some flowers in front of their household shrine in Kaligunj when Prakash had come to meet her. She remembered how hurtful his words were. She remembered every syllable he spoke but found to her relief that they hardly troubled her anymore. Why was she so sensitive to his words that particular evening? And, what had happened to Prakash at that hour? How strangely he behaved! And now, Prakash had gone home without even meeting her. That saddened her a little. The next moment, she was ashamed of being sad for Prakash not meeting her. And yet, was it not a normal thing for a family member to take leave of his relatives before parting? Uma breathed a sigh. She understood that Prakash avoided her intentionally because something was wrong—because he had spoken those wild words to her. Why did Prakash speak in that manner? Prakash and she had such a pleasant relationship, just like normal family members. That was broken forever.

'Uma, lunch is ready,' Surama called from the kitchen area. 'Come, let's eat.'

'Coming in a while, Ma.'

'Hurry up and bring along some drinking water for us.'

After they had eaten, they sat on the veranda, where Surama commenced her reading of the Ramayana. 'Today, we are at Sita's *vanavas*, her days in the forest. Listen. This chapter is beautiful but sad.'

Surama's reading of the evocative passages moved Uma with their sense of pathos. Just when Uma was absorbed in the scenes depicting Rama's unspoken remorse for Sita's ordeal, a maid interrupted them with the news of visitors.

'Let them be, Ma. Don't stop reading,' said Uma.

'Silly girl. Don't we have to meet our guests?'

'Oh, they are already here,' said Uma as Atul and a girl of Uma's age, approached.

Spreading out his hands Atul ran in to hug his Ma, Surama, who took him in her arms and tousled his hair. Looking at his companion, she said, 'Aren't you Mandakini, my child?'

Manda nodded as she bent down and touched Surama's feet.

'I call her "Didi",' announced Atul. Surama smiled, 'Do you? And, who is this person?' she asked pointing at Uma. 'The other didi Ma told me about,' he said.

'Dear Uma, do take Atul to see the monkeys,' said Surama.

Atul was not ready to leave his Ma so soon but was tempted when some other attractions around the monkeys were described to him.

When Atul and Uma had left, Surama held Mandakini's hand and asked her to sit. 'What is your Aunt Charu doing?'

'She is waiting for you at home. She has sent me to take you there.'

Surama liked the way Manda spoke—softly, gently.

'Do you know that I, too, am your aunt?'

'Yes, I do. Aunty Charu has spoken to me about you.'

'You are living with them only for the past few months. Had you met Charu before coming to them at Manikgunj?'

'No.'

It was not that Surama was unaware of these particulars. She was only trying to put Manda at ease with small talk.

'I met your father when he was staying with your uncle and aunt. He was a good man.'

Mandakini was quiet.

'Do you miss your father?'

'Yes, very much. He loved me dearly.'

'Did you spend a lot of time with him?'

'Not much. For some months when I was small and recently when he fell critically ill. I came to nurse him.'

'Who has brought you up, Manda?'

'My maternal grandmother. After she died, my maternal uncles took over the responsibility.'

'But didn't they want you back when your father passed away?'

'No.'

'Why?'

Mandakini looked down without answering.

Surama held her hand. 'Don't tell me if you do not wish to.'

Mandakini continued to look down but said, 'They said they did not want to take charge of a girl of marriageable age.'

'How was your life with them?'

'It was good. I could do all the work they wanted me to do. I did not mind working hard. The only thing I missed there was getting news of my father.'

'Do you like your new home in Manikgunj?'

'Yes, it is very pleasant there. My uncle and aunt are very kind and affectionate. Yet, I miss my days with my maternal uncles. During my stay with them, I lived with the hope that my father would come back. That hope has been completely shattered. All the comfort I have now cannot give me back that hope.'

'Don't be sad, Manda. Your father has gone to heaven.'

'Yes, I know. He was in great physical pain in his final days. He has now been relieved of that pain. He is in heaven.'

'And you have found a place where you are loved.'

'Yes.'

'I think Atul, too, is very fond of you.'

Manda nodded in agreement. She asked, 'Aunty, won't you come with me to see Charu Aunty?'

'Not today, Manda.'

'Charu Aunty has asked me to tell you that if it is more suitable for you, she can come over to your place instead of you visiting hers.'

'Then, Manda, let her, please, come to the Vishwanath temple tomorrow morning. I will be there to meet her. I will expect you to come there, too.'

'Aunty, I may not be able to come. I will stay back with

Atul at home. He does not like to be taken to crowded places.'

Surama called Uma to join them. Uma came, carrying Atul in her arms. The boy was in a hurry to get down and sit next to Surama.

'How have you come here, Manda?' asked Surama.

'Deven Babu drove us here. He is waiting outside in the car.'

'Oh, how careless of me! I must ask him to come in. And I must quickly arrange some refreshments for our guests.' She took Atul with her as she hurried away. The two young girls were left on their own.

Surama found that Devendra had brought his car closer to the gate of the house. He was calling out Atul's name to remind him that it was time to go home.

Using Atul as her messenger, Surama sent Deven an ardent request to come in and have something to eat. So Deven came into the outer room of the dwelling and accepted Surama's hospitality. Surama did not call her father to meet Deven, knowing that he would not like to see him. She had not invited Charu to her home precisely for that reason—to avoid displeasing Radhakishore.

The next morning, Uma and Surama went to pay their respects to Vishwanath with a servant. 'If you keep it for tomorrow, I can join you,' Radhakishore had proposed. But Surama had expressed a sudden desire to see Vishwanath that very morning.

Remembering how she had failed to pay obeisance to the god on her earlier visit, Surama asked for Vishwanath's forgiveness. However, the serene joy that comes to a person who is forgiven eluded her. Tears rolled down Uma's blue eyes in multiple drops as she bowed before the deity. Surama realized that Uma had been able to open her heart, that she had shared her plight with the god without reserve, which led to her being blessed with peace. Without letting her know, Surama lovingly blessed Uma.

They met Charu, who touched Surama's feet and received her blessings. 'Had never imagined that we would see each other like this,' said Charu. Atul was standing next to her. 'You have brought him, too?' asked Surama.

'He was very eager to come when he learned that you would be here. His father and Deven Dada have gone to Ramnagar today. Atul stayed back and accompanied me on this journey here.'

'Hasn't Manda come?'

'No, she didn't want to. She prefers staying at home.'

'She's a nice girl.'

'Yes. The poor thing has been devoid of love since she was a child.'

Surama introduced Uma to Charu. 'Uma Rani?' said Charu. 'Your ma had written to me about you. It is so nice to meet you.'

Uma smiled shyly.

'How long will you stay in Varanasi, Charu?'

'Probably for two months. I will not ask you to come home, of course, but will we be able to meet once in a while?'

'Why get close again, that too for just two months?'

'Can't we meet, sometimes, without getting close?'

'Let us meet, then, the way we have done today. Let me know when you visit Durga Bari or Batuk Bhairav. I will come to see you.'

'Okay.'

'And send Manda to see me, sometimes.'
'I will.'
They continued to talk about various topics, including Zamindar Radhakishore, the daily management of their places, Charu's health problems and Khuki. Both of them avoided speaking about Amar. After a while, they bid farewell to each other.

The very same evening, Charu sent Mandakini and Atul to visit Surama. Surama was a little annoyed at Charu's eagerness for an interaction, but when Atul interjected, 'Ma, I have caught Didi and brought her here, again,' she laughed and said, 'Good. You deserve a reward for that.'

After giving a gift to Atul, Surama called Uma. 'Here is your other didi,' she said.

As Atul wanted to be with his ma, Surama took him to watch the monkeys on the nearby trees, leaving Manda and Uma to chat with one another.

For a long time, they sat next to each other without speaking. Manda looked at Uma's sombre face a few times but kept quiet. Uma realized that she was expected to start a conversation, but she felt somewhat lost. She had no idea how to behave with a peer as she never had a friend of her own age. However, after some thought, she asked, 'Where is your paternal home, Uma?'

'Sorry, I cannot answer that, for I never had a fixed paternal home. My maternal uncles live in Kusumpur. I was brought up there.'

'Do you remember your mother?'

'No. I don't. She died when I was very small.'

'I'm sad to hear that,' said Uma with real sympathy. 'And your maternal uncles and aunts were not so good to you...'

'No, no, they were quite caring.'

'Then, why did Charu Aunty say that you have never really been loved?'

Mandakini did not mind answering Uma's foolish question. She smiled faintly and said, 'I think Charu Aunty said that because she herself is extremely affectionate.'

The simple-minded Uma went on, 'My ma, your Surama aunty, likes you a lot. She thinks rather highly of you.'

Manda looked at Uma and laughed a little. She said, 'I, on the other hand, hear *you* getting praised by Charu Aunty all the time. Indeed, her account of you makes me wish I were more like you.'

Uma was not sophisticated enough to deny that praise. She accepted the adulation smugly and came directly to her next question, 'Who do you think loves you more—your relatives in Kusumpur or Charu Aunty and her husband?'

Manda thought for a few seconds before answering, 'They all love me and are equally kind.'

'I know your life in Kusumpur was not easy. Your relatives made you work very hard. And, yet you say they were kind to you. Why?'

Mandakini's large, patient eyes rested on Uma's as she said, 'They looked after me after my mother's death; they have sheltered me for years. Even though my life was not very easy with them, I'm grateful for what they have done for me. I am sure they cared for me. I am equally grateful to Charu Aunty and her husband for giving me a home. They provide me with everything I need, and more. With them, I live in luxury. But suppose they did not look after me that well, would I be less indebted or less grateful? No.

People who shelter a destitute person like me, do that out of compassion.'

Uma's blue eyes had tears of sympathy in them. She moved closer to Manda and held one of her hands. 'You are large-hearted,' she said. Mandakini took Uma's other hand in her free one. 'Very generous of you to think so,' she said.

'Do you, occasionally, miss your people in Kusumpur?'

'I don't let myself miss them.'

'Why is that?'

'Because I had become a huge burden on them. When they used to express their frustration and anxiety at the difficulties I had brought into their lives, I hated myself. Thank God, a new home was found for me. My maternal relatives are rid of their burden at last.'

Uma was too innocent to grasp the significance of Mandakini's words. She asked, 'Why were they so burdened by you?'

Manda remained silent for a minute, before saying with a smile, 'Don't you realize it? It's the responsibility of a girl's guardians to marry her off when she reaches puberty.'

'Who was stopping them from marrying you off?'

'Who would accept me?'

'Why, what's wrong with you? Can't people see how beautiful you are?'

'That doesn't count because I am an orphan with no money. My parents didn't leave anything for me. Who would pay for my dowry?'

Uma reflected for a few seconds. Then, she said in a cheerful tone, 'Fortunately, nobody has to worry about you where you live now.'

'Not really. I am a burden to whoever takes charge of me.'

'That's sad. You must be keen to release your elders from that headache.'

'Yes, I am. But, is it possible to find a secure and permanent home for a cursed creature like me? I have now stopped thinking about my future. But I shouldn't be grumbling. Instead, I must thank God for placing me in the company of such wonderful people like Amar Uncle and Charu Aunty.'

Even though Uma didn't fully understand Manda's words, she sighed and said, 'I understand your distress.'

Manda was touched. She looked at Uma with admiration but did not say anything. Perhaps, she said in her mind, 'Immersed in tragedy yourself, you are still capable of feeling for others. You have one advantage, though. God has not given you the power to really miss what is lacking in your life.'

Two days later, Surama announced that she would have to go to Durga Bari that morning. 'Do come with me, Uma.'

'But, Ma, we visited that place just the other day.'

'Charu is coming there today. I want to meet her. Perhaps, Manda, too, will come. Won't you like to see Manda again?'

'Another time, Ma. Today I don't feel like going out.'

So, Surama left for Durga Bari alone.

Chapter 9

'Come, let us sit here and talk,' said Charu, pointing to the circular veranda on the premises of the Durga temple.

'Amid such a crowd? What will people think?' said Surama.

'Let people think what they like. We have no other way to be together.'

Knowing that was true, Surama complied. 'Hasn't Manda come with you?'

'No, she did not come. Since marriage proposals for her have started coming in, her uncle does not think it is fit for her to be in a public place. One proposal even seems suitable.'

'Is that so? Where is the boy from?'

'He is from this city. The family will come to see Manda once the negotiations are over.'

Surama was silent. She seemed to be reflecting on what she heard from Charu. Then she asked, 'How is the boy?'

'Quite likeable. But they are demanding a lot of dowry.'

'And you are fine with that?'

'What's the alternative? We have to get her married.'

'You could have waited for a while.'

'What's the use? She is already quite grown.'

'Will you consider it if I ask for her hand for a relative of mine?'

Charu's eyes widened. 'Is it for Prakash Uncle?'

'Yes.'

Happy and excited, Charu said, 'I hope you are not joking. Can Manda be so lucky?'

'Charu, I'm serious. But I need some time. Can the wedding wait for a while?'

'I will ask him. But I'm not sure if he will agree to that. He is looking forward to doing other things after Manda settles down. He wants to go to Rajputana as soon as he discharges his duties.'

'But, why Rajputana?' asked Surama, looking quite amused.

'Because he is quite fed up with his village. He wishes to buy a piece of land in Rajputana to build a nursing home on it.'

'Be with him wherever he goes.'

'Yes, I have to. He has become very careless about his health…'

'When you are in Rajputana, who will look after your zamindari?'

'Shyamacharan Uncle will be there. And Atul's father will visit the village whenever necessary.'

There were no other questions from Surama.

'Now, Didi, the matter we were speaking about. Are you really interested?'

'Yes, I am. I am quite looking forward to having Manda as Prakash's bride.'

'But you realize now that things can't wait. Will it be possible for you to schedule the wedding before the end of this month?'

'Don't worry. I can deal with that challenge. But will Manda's primary guardian agree to the match?'

'You mean Atul's father? I have no doubt that he would. He knows how good a groom Prakash Uncle would make for Manda. Now, the guardian of the bride needs to meet the guardian of the groom to complete all the formalities. They will need to decide the dowry and the date for the ceremony.'

Charu's dramatic delivery made Surama laugh. She said, 'Of course, talks between the two parties should take place. My father is the groom's guardian. From your side, as a representative of the actual guardian of the bride, please send his friend Deven Babu to meet my dad. We can decide on the dowry right now. My demand is huge—the girl with all her individuality. Nothing less than that will do.'

Charu responded with a bright smile.

The conversation came to an end as Tiwari, Charu's attendant, arrived with a wailing Atul. The child complained that a band of ungrateful monkeys, after eating all the roasted chickpeas he had given them, had snatched away his little ivory-topped walking stick. He said in a disgruntled tone that the attendant and the maid were unhelpful in retrieving his stick from those naughty simians.

Surama managed to console the child.

'Will you be here for a long time, Madam?' Tiwari asked Charu. Surama answered for her, 'No, Tiwari, we will all go home now.' As Surama stood up, Charu, too, got ready to leave.

Surama enquired, 'Charu, how shall we come to know about the response of Manda's Uncle?'

'I'll send a written message with Tiwari tomorrow morning.

Should have preferred to come to you myself, but Manda's Uncle teases me for wanting to see you again and again. He says, "This great pilgrimage of ours has unexpectedly turned out to be a great grand pilgrimage for you!"'

Surama blushed and replied, 'No wonder he grumbles! Instead of going to important places with him, all you want to do is be with me.'

'I don't like gallivanting around the city like him.'

'And, Charu, I would like to speak with Manda, too. Can you send her to see me tomorrow?'

'Why, Didi, do you want to follow the European practice of wanting the girl's consent?'

'Yes.'

∞

Radhakishore was getting ready for his evening walk. He was very pleased to see Manda when she stood upright after touching his feet. 'Is this the girl you were telling me about, Surama? I've no doubt that she is a nice girl.'

'Then, you have no objection to the match, Baba?'

'No, I don't. The only difficulty is that we have to hurry a bit. But we will manage. If somebody from their side can come to meet me tomorrow, I can finalize the date of the wedding.'

Radhakishore was especially happy with that proposal for Prakash's marriage due to a deeply personal reason. His daughter's humiliation in her marital home had, all through the long years, kept him as humiliated as she was supposed to feel. That people from that haughty family would have to approach him, the guardian of the groom, with humility gave him a great sense of satisfaction.

Surama had been sure of her father's approval, but his positive words still pleased her. She fervently prayed that no further obstacles would come up to stop the two young people from uniting. And, she felt that sooner or later, Prakash would be happy with Manda.

The two parties completed their negotiations soon, and the date of the ceremony was fixed. Amar avoided meeting his father-in-law due to a persistent feeling of embarrassment. Devendra acted as his representative at every step leading up to the event.

Within a few weeks, the wedding day was approaching rapidly, although the groom was still in Taherpur. He had written to his cousin, the zamindar, that he could only reach Varanasi by train on the morning of his wedding day as he had some urgent work to attend to in Taherpur.

Surama had not mentioned to Uma that Prakash was getting married, but the girl must have heard about the wedding from other sources. Although traditionally the groom's family played a lesser role in the main proceedings of the ceremony than the bride's, there was still plenty of activity and a constant stream of people coming and going in Radhakishore's Varanasi home in preparation for the event. As a result, the name 'Prakash' was frequently mentioned. Every time Uma heard that name, she felt a sharp pain in her heart. As the days went by, she withdrew more and more from the life around her. She tried to hide herself in a corner. She had almost stopped speaking to anybody, and she looked physically weakened.

Noticing her sad eyes and her strange behaviour, Surama was worried. She had not expected Uma to get so deeply affected by the new developments. What if the poor girl broke down before the wedding guests or before Prakash himself?

The day before the ceremony, Surama approached her father and said, 'A group of people I know are going to Vrindavan by tonight's train to attend an auspicious festival. Baba, please allow Uma and me to join them.'

Radhakishore was taken aback. What kind of request was that? An important family function was going to take place the next day. How can things be managed without Surama?

Finding her father so upset, the daughter changed her approach. She reminded the zamindar that the bride's family might look for her during the ceremonies and could even invite her to their house as she was technically still Amar Mitra's first wife. By going away to Vrindavan, she would save the groom's side from humiliation. The argument was so persuasive that Radhakishore wholeheartedly approved of the journey to Vrindavan.

Uma was a little surprised when she was informed that she would be making a train journey to Vrindavan in a few hours. She was, however, not averse to the idea.

A senior employee of Radhakishore, a bodyguard and the maid—all three peeved at having to miss the wedding festivities—accompanied Surama and Uma to another holy city.

Before leaving for the railway station, Surama sent a letter to Charu. She wrote:

Dear Charu,

Please don't be surprised at my absence. A sudden development has compelled me to take this course of action. I'm sure Prakash wouldn't mind if I don't attend his wedding. He knows me well enough to understand that I wouldn't do this without a reason. Many relatives and friends will surely criticize me for this. I entreat you to not be one of them. I will meet you after returning from Vrindavan. I don't want to go back to Kaligunj without seeing you once more.

Surama wrote another note and left it for Prakash.

Tomorrow is your wedding day, but we are leaving for Vrindavan today. I will see you when all the festivities are over. A judge may pass a death sentence. But, does he wish to be present at the execution? The second reason for our absence, as you would have correctly surmised, is the need to save Uma from unnecessary pain, which she is bound to experience when she sees you dressed as a groom for another. I know that you, too, would prefer not to see her at this time. I am greatly obliged to you for honouring your promise, and that too in such a short period of time. God is sure to forgive you wholeheartedly. He will shower His blessings on you. You may have strong objections to getting married to a girl not of your own choice. But what you now consider the chains of a prisoner will, by His grace, one day turn into garlands of flowers. May God give you peace and happiness.

Chapter 10

As soon as the wedding celebrations were over, Devendra urged Amar to return to Manikgunj. 'I've had enough of this region of chickpea-flour eaters,' he said.

'Why? Is it giving you indigestion?'

'Oh no. We are all digesting our meals quite well here. Actually, that's the problem. Look at your bloated belly. It makes you look like a typical zamindar.'

'What's the harm in that? And have you noticed how even our Charu has gained weight?'

'Yes, Charu has got her strength back. However, that's no reason for our continuing to be here.'

'True. But I am fed up with my village. It is high time I shift to another place and seriously devote myself to medical practice and social work.'

Devendra grinned. 'Serious work doesn't suit everybody, especially prosperous people like you who have helpers to attend to your every need. I remember watching three attendants running to you with comforters to soothe your minor cold!'

'I disagree with you. I mean, prosperous people with personal attendants can also work hard at their jobs.'

'We have to see. Anyway, when are we going back to Manikgunj?'

Charu had entered the room and was listening to the

friends' conversation. She said, 'We are not going before Didi comes back from her pilgrimage. She wants to see me before leaving for Kaligunj.'

'What? You want us to wait here for your didi like *chatak*[26] birds?' said Amar, teasingly.

'As if meeting Didi is a dishonourable thing,' said Charu, miffed.

'Do you think it is honourable?'

'Yes, I do. Explain to me how it is not.'

'I don't want to argue with you. Wait here for as long as you want to. Just spare me your squabbles.'

Tiwari entered the room, carrying a letter. '*Chitthi*,' he announced in his usual rustic accent.

'Is that your sweet summons?' joked Amar.

'Stop teasing me,' said Charu as she took the letter from Tiwari. It was addressed to her.

After reading a part of it, she got up to leave the room. Still peeved with her husband, she called, 'Tiwari ji, please call a cab for me.'

'Charu, where do you want to go? Who has sent the letter? What does it say?'

'It is none of your business. I have to go and meet one of Manda's in-laws,' said Charu, indirectly referring to Surama.

'I see. It seems you like this new relationship better…'

'Yes. Because the old one got destroyed in some mysterious fire.'

---

[26]'Chataks' are swallows. According to Indian mythology, these birds have holes in their throats through which water can ooze out. As a result, they have to wait for rain so that water falling from above, bypassing those holes, can quench their thirst.

Amar did not comment on that. He tried to concentrate on the book he was reading.

Surama had come back from Vrindavan and was planning to return to Kaligunj in a few days. She wanted to meet Charu before that. Apart from the helpers, she and Uma were the only people present at their residence in Varanasi. She had invited Charu to her home.

Amarnath did not stop Charu from taking a cab and meeting her didi.

∞

The conversation revolved around Manda and Prakash's wedding. At one point, Charu said, 'Prakash Uncle looked grim and aloof during the ceremonies. Maybe he doesn't find Manda suitable for him...'

Surama responded, 'Don't be silly. How can Prakash not be happy to have Manda?' Then, she added, 'I half expected you all to have left this place for home.'

'I wouldn't have gone. Remember, you had said you wished to see me on your return from the pilgrimage. Anyway, when did you come back?'

'This morning. By train.'

'You had given me the impression that the two of you would be away only for three or four days. What took you so long? Weren't you missing the wedding ceremonies in Varanasi?'

'Performing the holy rituals in Vrindavan took more time than I had expected. My father must be furious with me for not attending the *boubhat*.[27] It has been four days since that ceremony.'

---

[27] A Bengali post-wedding ceremony in which a bride cooks and serves food to her in-laws for the first time.

'By the way, when are you leaving Varanasi?'

'Haven't planned yet. Now that all the post-wedding functions are also over, there's no harm in staying back here for a few more days. Tell me, when do *you* want me to go?'

'You will listen to me? How fortunate I am today!'

'Baba will be angry with me if I go now or two days later. So, let us give this place two more days.'

'Lovely! Then, we can even go to Ramnagar together. I have not been to Ramnagar. Would be nice to go there with you. Can you come?'

'Yes, I can. But...'

'But what?'

'We need to know when we are starting and who else is going. When your programme for the outing is fixed, send me a message.'

'Right, Didi. And you know, Didi, we have bought a new house in Varanasi.'

'Really? Where?'

'Beside Asi River. Won't you come and see the place?'

'One by one. First, let us visit Ramnagar.'

The next day they went to Ramnagar with Devendra. Amar stayed back. Charu, in her irritation, kept on grumbling to her didi about Amar's lazy habits and bad manners. Surama remarked, 'That's why I had said "but".'

'I don't understand. He is not your elder brother-in-law.'[28]

'Yet, more remotely related.'

'All this is beyond my comprehension,' sighed Charu, exasperated.

---

[28] In Indian tradition, it is expected that a woman would respect her husband's elder brother almost as highly as she does her father-in-law.

'How can you know?' Surama whispered to herself.

Charu looked at Uma and said, 'Uma Rani, you are coming to see the new house we bought, aren't you?'

Uma looked at Surama for an answer. Charu said, 'Do you have to take permission from Ma all the time? Am I not your aunty?'

Uma smiled. 'I did not say that I am not coming.'

Charu said, 'Won't you both come, Didi?'

'When?' asked Surama.

'Tomorrow. Tomorrow is an auspicious day. So, we have decided to hold a house-warming tomorrow. We will keep it very simple, though. I, on behalf of Manda's family, invite you both to join us. Come and see Manda's people.'

Surama was a little hurt by Charu's strange manner of addressing her and Uma. She urged, 'Don't use such harsh words, Charu.'

'Sorry, Didi, that was only out of my frustration at your refusal to be with us.'

'Charu, we are scheduled to take the night train for Kaligunj, tomorrow. Otherwise, we could have joined you.'

'Our function is in the morning, Didi. Do come. I assure you there will be plenty of time for you to catch your train. But, Didi, do not leave Varanasi so soon. Give me a few more days to come and visit you. Perhaps this is the last time we can see each other.'

The last time we can see each other.

Surama couldn't shake off the echoes of those words ringing in her ears. What was the harm, she thought, in having a little fun, just to carry some pleasant memories with her? What she had resolved to do with her life would never change. A short diversion, surely, would not make any difference to that journey. She might regret it later if she did not take that chance. It might actually be a good thing to quench her innermost desire to see and hear Amar once. Even though no one would gain or lose anything from that, the constant waves of sorrow in her heart would finally have a few moments of joy bubbling up to the surface. Her thirsty eyes would get a sweet draught and her worthless longings would be fulfilled.

Finding Surama silent, Charu asked, 'Won't you come?'

'Are you sure there won't be any trouble if I am there?'

'Of course, I am sure! You are the one who is an expert at making trouble. Do not try to accuse others. After dropping us off at the new house, the car will come here to pick you up and Uma. Come early, Didi, okay.'

'We will.'

At home, Charu excitedly reported to Amar how Surama had agreed to attend the house-warming. Was not that wonderful?

Finding Amarnath unimpressed, she asked, 'How can you just be sitting there after hearing that? Don't we have to make arrangements?'

'Tell me what should we do: greet her with a *roshanchouki* or hire a gora's orchestra?'[29]

'How can you be so flippant? It irritates me. Remember, Didi will be among us after months. Don't we need to give her a proper welcome?'

'Why did she suddenly change her mind?'

'I don't know. You ask her.'

---

[29] 'Roshanchouki' is a serenade of shehnai and accompanying instruments.

'I don't think she is serious. She agreed to come just to please you.'

'Of course not. She promised me she would come. Hope you do not run away from the house.'

'What do you mean?'

'You might avoid meeting her and that could give rise to some kind of scandal. In fact, that is the reason for Didi's reluctance to come over to our place. She fears that you would run away, leaving people to talk.'

Amar was about to say something in an unguarded moment, but he checked himself. Charu said, 'Come, let us start making the arrangements.'

'Tell me, how you want it to be. I'll ask Deven to do everything for you.'

'Are you determined to not get involved?'

'What can you expect from a lazy person like me?'

After dinner, Amar picked up a book to read and reclined on a couch next to an open window. The world outside, soaked in moonlight, was smiling. The sharp, cool winter breeze, coming through the window, made him shiver slightly, but the moonlight was too soothing for him to leave his perch. His book lay open as he looked at the garden below. The gravelly soil of Varanasi had prevented the flower plants from thriving. Tired of the strong sunshine throughout the day, they seemed to relax under the mildness of the moonbeams. The main city of Varanasi, just a short distance away, was getting less and less noisy. Amar suddenly felt as if an enormous net of illusion was spreading around him.

Entering the room, Devendra took a seat near his friend. 'What are you up to?' he asked. His reverie broken, Amar, pointing to his book, said, 'The usual thing. And, what about you?'

'Don't ask me, Brother. I am quite in a soup.'

'Why? What happened?'

'I completed the shopping for Charu according to her list, but she is now criticizing me for the poor quality and high prices of the items. The poor girl is so excited to welcome her didi tomorrow that she completely forgot to have mercy on me.'

Amar grinned in amusement.

'And even you have no sympathy for me,' continued Deven. 'No wonder, you laugh. Tomorrow is the day slated for your promotion to the status of Lord Vishnu with your twin consorts of Lakshmi and Saraswati.'

Giving his friend an affectionate push, Amar said, 'What rubbish!' But Devendra went on, 'Just tell me one thing, Brother, why does she avoid coming here—a place that so warmly awaits her? Is it because the man is slightly queer or something...?'

'Ask that from your sister, Charu. See how angry she gets if you try to find fault with me. She might start beating you, even.'

'If nobody is at fault, why is the situation like this? There must be a reason... Tell me about it.'

'I will someday.'

'Oh, I understand. The conclusion of your life's saga, sorry, farce, is tomorrow. You want to keep me in suspense until then. Just tell me, is it a tragedy or a comedy?'

'Is it not your bedtime? Aren't you sleepy? I can hardly keep my eyes open.'

'Okay. Goodnight, then. See you tomorrow.'

As scheduled, they reached their new house quite early in the day. Their car was, then, sent to bring Surama and Uma from their residence. Expecting the car to return anytime soon, Charu kept her eyes on the gate as she shelled peas. Amar was upstairs at a window. Pretending to examine the quality of its shutters, he surreptitiously looked down at the road now and then. The pedestrians he could see there appeared to him like figures on a surreal screen.

There was a noise of wheels as the sedan stopped at the gate. Instinctively, Amar looked away. But in his mind's eye, he could see her—an austere *yogini*,[30] attired in a taintless raw-silk sari, loose locks of hair tumbling over her back, standing mutely at the door of the car.

Deven hurried towards the vehicle as soon as he suspected that there was no one inside it except the driver. He could only see Tiwari, in his *pugree*,[31] through the open door.

'They were not home, Sir. The ladies have left for their village, leaving this letter with a servant,' said Tewari while handing an envelope to Deven. In his agitation, Devendra opened it himself. The note addressed to Charu said:

Dear Charu,

Forgive me. Have to leave for Kaligunj immediately. Wish your house-warming a grand success. Rejoice in it on my behalf, too. Tell me all about it when you write to me.

Your Didi

---

[30] A female practitioner of yoga, someone who has achieved a certain degree of mastery over yogic practices.
[31] A type of headgear, typically a long piece of cloth, wrapped around the head as a turban.

Chapter 11

Surama reached Kaligunj with Uma. She had utilized the time during her long journey by analysing her thoughts meticulously. For, she felt guilty—enormously guilty—and yet was unable to pinpoint the source of her guilt. She was thoroughly frustrated by the indistinct and confused nature of her emotions. She could feel the heat but not detect the fire.

At last, exhausted by self-searching, she returned to her interest in other people's problems.

When she reached home, she found her father seriously offended by her overstaying in Vrindavan. Prakash had gone back to Taherpur, taking Manda with him. For a few moments, Surama regretted not returning earlier, but as soon as her eyes fell on Uma, she knew that avoiding the festivities at home had spared the innocent girl some pain.

For a few seconds, she thought Uma did not deserve all that sympathy. That perplexed Surama. She became aware of the strange mood swings inside her. She remembered how unkindly she had behaved with Charu before leaving Varanasi. After accepting Charu's invitation to join in the house-warming, she had left the city merely leaving a note behind. Yet, Surama did not really blame herself for that. She had taken that step after prolonged reflection. A sudden longing to see Amar had risen in her heart, which she later decided to ignore. Was not her separation from Amar permanent? Then, where was the room for such silly wishes?

Her complex emotions scared Surama. The desire to meet Amar, even if only to hear a few words from him, was making her life miserable. Despite all her struggles against it, a sensation of regret at her own stubbornness had begun to gnaw at her heart, threatening to make her years as a single woman bereft of any nobility. It was good that she had run away from that family get-together before finding herself in what, she now thought, would have been a laughable situation.

Fortunately, that matter was now closed. That she had given Charu a shabby treatment hardly mattered to either Charu or herself. Surama was forever guilty of not repaying Charu adequately for her unconditional love, and she knew that Charu would soon forgive her wholeheartedly as she always did.

The real problem was her inner conflicts. One part of her mind approved of the way she conducted her life while another part was acutely critical. Worse, she felt as if she could hear a faint voice inside her constantly accusing her of something—something she was incapable of specifying.

With his household running smoothly again, under Surama's management, Radhakishore forgot that he was ever angry with his daughter.

Uma looked content with her regular tasks of caring for the family deity, performing the rituals connected with His worship and doing other necessary housework. Surama, too, had her daily routine of work. Outwardly, nothing had changed for her, but inwardly, she had begun to experience a strange upheaval. She woke up every morning full of expectations, though she did not know what it was that she expected. No matter how active she remained through the day, her heart was waiting for something to happen. With half of her mind, she kept alert for a signal from outside—a signal that would make her happy. She went to bed at night feeling heavy with sadness at the futility of the day, which did not bring the message she was waiting for. What was the meaning of it all? She was leading the life she had chosen, leaving no scope for change. Then, why was she yearning for novelty?

Many months had passed after Prakash and Manda's wedding. Surama did not hear from Charu after that unpleasant incident in Varanasi.

In Taherpur, Prakash had managed to put the administrative problems of that part of the zamindari in order. Radhakishore's business as a landholder was running smoothly, on the whole. So, the thought of retirement came to the zamindar's mind. 'Dear Surama,' he said one day, 'Now that Prakash no longer needs to be personally present in Taherpur, I am thinking of calling him home. He can regulate the whole of our zamindari from here. You, too, are an excellent manager. Let me retire now and spend my last days in Varanasi. Age is taking a toll on my health. Varanasi would be good for me…'

'But, Baba, I cannot let you go to Varanasi and live there all by yourself. I will come with you,' said Surama.

'Child, you are not old enough to get detached from the world.'

Surama smiled to herself. Was not she already detached from the world? However, to her father, she only said, 'Baba, wherever you choose to live is my world. Your well-being is all that I care for.'

'Then, be with me in Varanasi as long as I live. But after that come back and devote your time for the betterment of our business.'

Not getting any reply from Surama, Radhakishore went on, 'Can't I expect that the younger members of my family—you and Prakash—would work towards upholding the prestige of our name?'

When Surama promised to act as her father wished, arrangements for their moving to Varanasi began in earnest. Prakash, instructed to come home, arrived in Kaligunj with Manda.

Surama was genuinely curious about Manda's attitude to life. So, she began to speak more intimately with her.

'When in Taherpur, did you remember me sometimes, Manda?'

'Yes, Aunty...'

'Perhaps you remember me as someone who snatched you from the loving embrace of your uncle and aunt and banished you to the jungle.'

Manda bent down and touched Surama's feet. With a tremble in her voice, she said, 'How can you accuse me of that, Aunty? In fact, I always remember you with the deepest of gratitude. I will never be able to repay you for what you have given me.'

'Do you really think so, Manda?'

'Yes, Aunty. You got me a secure and comfortable sanctuary...'

Surama took hold of the younger girl's hand and said, 'Are you happy, Manda? Does Prakash realize what a gem of a girl you are? Has he learnt to take care of you?'

'Don't worry for me, Aunty. You people have given me

shelter at your feet. What more can I wish for?'

'I am not satisfied with that answer, Manda. Tell me, does Prakash attend to your needs?'

Manda looked down. She said, 'The person you are speaking of cannot take care of himself. How can we expect him to look after others? I am worried about his health. He adores you. Will you, please, ask him to not ignore his health? My only wish is that he keeps well.' Manda's voice was deep and convincing. Surama realized how keenly the young girl desired her husband's well-being. She was surprised. How could a girl, barely in her early teens, equate her own happiness with that of her husband—that, too, so soon after their marriage? Where did she learn to feel that way? What kind of commitment was required to achieve that state of mind?

Nobody had told Surama that only abundant and unconditional love for another human being could give rise to such an attitude.

Soon it was close to the day of Surama's departure for Varanasi with her father and Uma. Every member of the staff of the zamindari was sad that their master and his daughter were leaving them, maybe for good.

Finding Manda downcast and genuinely unhappy at the impending separation, Surama said, 'Dear Manda, why are you so sad? The person you have devoted your life to, will be with you. So, why do I see tears in your eyes?'

Manda said, 'I don't remember my mother, Ma, but feel as if *you* are that person. When my husband and I were asked to be back in Kaligunj, I expected that we would all live together in this house. ...I will really miss you when you are gone.'

Manda's words had brought a tear to Surama's eye, but she quickly brushed it away and composed herself. Manda had noticed Uma standing next to her in silence for a few seconds before scurrying away. The newly married girl guessed that Uma was curious about her life in Taherpur but was hesitating to begin a conversation. So, one day Manda approached Uma and, taking the girl's hand in her own, asked, 'Have you forgotten me, Uma?'

'No,' said Uma, warmly extending her other hand and holding Manda's.

Manda said, 'In Taherpur, I remembered you and Ma so frequently. Uma, are you going to Varanasi, too?'

'Yes.'

'Can't you stay back?'

'No. I want to be with Ma.'

'Remember me when you are there.'

Uma nodded.

On the day of their departure, Surama met Prakash privately. 'Are you well, Prakash?'

'Yes, very well. Thank you. And how are you all?'

'Fine. Uma is happy. She likes Varanasi better than this place.'

Prakash looked at the ground, thoughtfully. Looking up, he said, 'May God always keep her well and happy.'

'May God grant you everlasting happiness, too,' said Surama.

'Don't I look extremely happy already?' asked Prakash in a faintly sad voice.

'Yes, you do,' said Surama, ignoring the hint of sarcasm in Prakash's words. 'Take good care of Manda. She is a gem of a girl and a blessing from God to you. She has only one wish in her life—to see you happy. Learn to value her. Learn to love her.'

Prakash looked down again. After pausing for a few seconds, he said, 'I know how wonderful she is... However, what you have done is akin to binding a scoundrel with a golden chain.'

'No, I did not do that. One day you will realize that she is not a constraint but a source of joy in your life.'

'I will try to believe that. Bless me that I can.'

Chapter 12

They were in Varanasi again. Surama remembered the pleasant days of her earlier stay in Varanasi about a year ago. How she treasured the memories of those few weeks! But six long months had passed after the family had come there, again, leaving Surama as joyless as she was in her village in Bengal. The delightful Varanasi of her previous stay seemed to have dropped from the Earth, altogether, and was nestled in her own heart! During her earlier stay, praying before Vishwanath's idol was like visiting a live god, but now she encountered only a stump of stone covered with flowers and bel leaves. Who would, now, accept her tenderly arranged offerings on a puja platter?

It was a monsoon evening. River Bhagirathi overflowed its banks. The sky was overcast. Countless little lamps were glowing in the ghats and temples of Varanasi. The sound of bells and gongs announced that the aarti was in progress in the places of worship. River Ganges, bordering the city, flowed with deep dignity and power. The water looked grey and so did the sky above. Small, riverside temples, partially submerged by the seasonal rise of the water level of the Ganges, held up their steeples to mark their existence. While the temples remained noisy, much of the riverside was quiet and peaceful. A short distance away, a pyre at the cremation ground flickered as the fire gradually diminished.

Radhakishore and Uma were engaged in their evening prayers. Surama, who preferred to pray indoors, was watching the dying crematory fire, which gave off sparks from time to time.

Surama mused that life itself was like a pyre, with the first sparks igniting a tiny flame that grew steadily bigger with each passing year. For a number of years, the flame burnt bright. But, ultimately, life ended in a handful of ash, which was later integrated into the immensity of the universe. Her father, in his sixties; young Uma with her tiny hopes, desires, joys and miseries; bright and handsome Prakash; poor Manda; and she herself, now aged twenty-seven, her life riddled with problems—all of them were destined to meet the same end. A few fistfuls of ash is what would remain of them.

By and by, the sounds of the aarti stopped. The zamindar said, 'Let's go home now. It's getting late...'

Home was just a short distance away. After reaching there, Surama lost no time in getting ready for her evening prayers. As she had seated herself and was about to begin, Uma called her to say, 'Ma, here is a letter for you.'

'A letter for me? Are you sure?'

'Yes. Your name is written on it.'

'Then, keep it there. Will read it later.'

After Uma left, Surama got up, closed the door of her room, took the envelope and tried to decipher in whose hand the address was written. The light of the puja lamp was too dim for her to be sure, but she thought it was Charu's writing. However, she was not inclined to read the missive immediately.

After her puja, Surama helped Uma in preparing the

zamindar's evening meal, waited for the girl to eat her simple widow's fare, and got their household help and other employees to have their dinner. 'When are *you* going to dine, Ma?' asked Uma. 'After I read that letter,' said Surama.

In the privacy of her bedroom, she opened the envelope and was surprised to find that it was not from Charu but from Prakash, written from Kaligunj.

It was a year now that Surama, Radhakishore and Uma were living in Varanasi. Prakash and Surama had not corresponded during that period. What made him write to her suddenly? Surama rebuked herself for expecting to hear from Charu for it was Surama, herself, who was trying to break their bond.

Prakash had written:

Dear Surama,

Hope you are not offended with me for not writing to you for all these months. From Dada's letters I get to know that you are well. That keeps me satisfied.

I write to you today because I am in trouble and have only you to share my worry and frustration with. Manda is seriously ill. I do not know what to do. Can you come over? Of course, you must discuss the matter with Dada before taking any decision.

Regards,
Prakash

Uma had come there and was standing nearby. Looking at Surama's grave and thoughtful face, she wondered what the contents of the letter could be. Knowing how eager Uma was for the information, Surama related it to her. 'That was from Prakash. He writes to say Manda is critically ill. He probably fears for her life.'

Uma turned pale. 'What's the illness?'

'Prakash has not written that. He wants me to go there after discussing the matter with your Dadababu.'

After Surama left to meet the zamindar, Uma was lost in thought. She remembered how fondly Manda had interacted with her, how she had urged Uma not to forget her. But Uma had intentionally tried to forget Manda, for whenever she remembered her, there was a kind of ache in Uma's heart. For the past two years, Uma had kept Manda out of her mind. She was pleased to note, however, that that twitch of pain associated in her mind with Manda had gone. Uma had healed or had almost healed. After knowing how ill Manda was, Uma, in fact, felt guilty for not reciprocating Manda's warmth—for falsely promising the other teenager that she would honour their friendship. Now, she wished with all her heart that Manda should not die. 'What did Dadababu say?' she asked as soon as Surama came after meeting her father.

'He asked me to go there tomorrow. He wanted to come with me, but I told him not to as he is not keeping too well these days.'

'How serious is Manda's illness, Ma? I hope she doesn't die.'

'Do you want to come along with me, Uma?'

'Do I need to?' asked Uma, a little worried.

Surama understood the cause of her reluctance. She had observed how Uma had slowly recovered from her emotional pain. She had also noticed how the experience had reshaped her personality. Or maybe, it was merely her growing up—her passing through puberty—that had given her maturity and made her better understand the world around her. Whatever it might be, Surama decided Uma was not yet ready for a platonic relationship with Prakash. So, she said, 'You stay back, Uma. Your dadababu will need you. I will call you in case Manda's condition worsens.'

'Right. Just tell Manda that...'

'That what?'

'That I will never forget her again. I wonder if she still remembers me.'

'I'll ask her,' said Surama, putting her hand on Uma's head and caressing her. 'But I'm sure she remembers you.'

Chapter 13

A month had passed by after Surama came to be with Manda and Prakash. Manda's recovery was gradual, as slow as a summer-ravaged creeper reviving with daily sprinkling of water. In Prakash's keenness to get his wife back to health, Surama discerned his growing affection for her and believed that it was in response to Manda's single-minded devotion to him. As she watched Prakash and Manda beginning to enjoy each other's company, she understood why she herself had never found happiness in her life. It occurred to her that however accomplished one might be, one could not achieve anything without God's blessings. For that, one had to rise above one's arrogance and conceit and accept what God had meant one to be.

She was about to enter Manda's room to give her the afternoon measure of medicine. She, however, halted at the door when she noticed Prakash sitting close to his wife's bed. He was turning the pages of a book. Moving away from the door, she stood at the window, out of sight of the couple. She was gripped by a strong desire to eavesdrop on their conversation.

Mandakini's face, though pale, had an unmistakable expression of contentment and pride as she watched Prakash from her bed.

As the clock struck four, Prakash sat erect in his chair

and said, 'Time to give you the medicine.'

'Yes,' said Manda, softly. 'Ma will soon come for that.'

'Why wait for her? Let me give it to you today.'

'This one is a little complicated. Two or three ingredients have to be combined together. Ma can mix them easily.'

'I know. But I want to do it today.'

Realizing that Prakash was really keen, Manda did not resist any further.

Surama moved away from the window. Breathing a sigh of relief, she went to her room to complete the letter she was writing to her father. When she met Prakash, next, much later in the evening, he asked, 'Did somebody tell you...?'

'What?' asked Surama, losing colour.

'Don't get nervous. It's only that I received a letter from Manikgunj a while ago.'

'I see,' said Surama, calming down somewhat but still feeling tense. 'Hope everybody is well there. Whose letter is it?'

'Manda's uncle, Amar Babu's.'

'They want her to be there?'[32]

'You are right. They were in Rajputana for many months. As I did not know their address in Rajputana, I had written to them in Manikgunj. They found my letter only after their return a few days back. Concerned that Manda is not well, Amar Babu has offered to send a reliable person to take her there for treatment. I posted a reply to Amar Babu immediately, saying that he need not send anyone. That I myself will take her there, but only for a short visit, when

---

[32]It was a tradition in Indian families that if a married girl fell ill, the responsibility for her treatment had to be borne by her maiden family.

she is a little better. I can easily spare a few days from my work at this time of the year.'

'You have done the right thing, Prakash. I am sure they would be really pleased to see Manda.'

Touched by the news that her uncle and aunt were concerned about her and wished to have her with them, Manda became extremely eager to visit Manikgunj. 'I am well enough for travel now and can't wait for the day when I am with Uncle and Aunty,' were her excited words, repeated again and again in Surama and Prakash's presence.

'Dear Prakash, as Manda is so keen to go there, why delay? It would be a good thing if you two make a visit there soon. I feel she is well enough for travel. Her relatives there would be so pleased to see her,' said Surama.

'When do *you* plan to go back to Varanasi, Surama?'

'Not very soon.'

'Then, you'll be all alone here when we two are away.'

'That doesn't matter.'

'No, no. I can't leave you alone here. We can go to Manikgunj a few days later.'

'Actually, Prakash, I have decided to be here for a longer stay. So, no point in delaying your trip for my sake.'

'Won't the family miss you in Varanasi? For how long can they manage without you?'

'I have no worry about them. My father will be well looked after by Uma, and Lord Vishwanath, at whose feet Uma has found her rightful place, will look after her.'

Prakash looked thoughtful for a moment. His eyes were fixed on the ground. Then, he met Surama's gaze and said, 'May she always remain happy at His feet.'

Prakash's face was unclouded and sincere. Its expression

told Surama that her relative was making a laudable effort to get over his weakness for Uma. It pleased her.

'Why wait, then? You can go to Manikgunj tomorrow itself,' she said.

'And you will be all alone here?'

'How does that matter?'

Prakash remained meditative, again, for a while. Then he asked hesitantly, 'May I ask you something?'

'What?'

'I am a little scared to put that question to you...'

'Don't make a fuss. Tell me straight away what you want to say.'

'Why don't you come to Manikgunj with us?'

Surama shivered. 'Me? Where?'

'To Manikgunj.'

Manikgunj? Was Prakash making fun of her? If she had a place there, why was she looking for a spot to call home somewhere, anywhere, in the immensity of this planet? How could she go there? Didn't she have any shame? Had she not pushed away the love and affection she had received there? She had no honourable way of going back now. Not only had she broken the relationship with the people in that house, but she had also deeply hurt its inmates with her words and actions, not caring even for a façade of good manners. No, she had no right to pollute that place with her presence.

As Surama was not saying anything, Prakash asked again, 'Won't you come with us? Is there any harm if you do?'

'Any harm? You mean you are really considering my going there?'

'Yes. You can come back with us. A visit like that can

always be done. Even Amar Babu had come here once.'

'You say there is no harm?'

'Yes. I do.'

'You think nobody would take offence if I landed there?'

'Why should anybody take offence?'

'Nobody would say that I had no business there?'

Prakash could not help laughing before he said, 'Impossible. Nobody will ask you such a hurtful question. On the contrary, I am sure, they will be immensely pleased to see you again.'

'You don't know, Prakash, how badly I behaved with them in Varanasi. Having accepted their invitation to meet them, I ran away without notice—left the city altogether without telling them. Charu stopped writing to me after that.'

'Well, when you meet them this time, I am sure you can apologize for that.'

'That was only one of the instances of my ill-treatment of them. There are several others.'

'Ask their forgiveness for all of them on this visit. I know how you loved them and cared for them. Why, unnecessarily, leave them bitter?'

Surama was excited by Prakash's words—by the possibilities they suggested. The sudden optimism rendered her childlike. As if tired of her own thinking, she put all her trust in Prakash's reasoning. To a person who feels lost, words showing a way out of their troubles might sound like an oracle. The import of Prakash's words had the same effect on Surama. She stopped using her own intelligence. 'You can still go there' was the phrase that rang in her ears. Her heart said, 'Go there and seek forgiveness. Excessive arrogance does not suit you. Do not forget that you are a woman. You are breaking down internally. Do not pretend that you are not. You were unkind to them. The time has come to say sorry.' In the core of her soul, she felt that she would be forgiven as Amar and Charu were large-hearted people.

Dealing with so many varied though connected sensations at the same time had made her approach to the matter at hand haphazard. Consequently, her responses to Prakash's appeals were like childish gestures.

When Surama had not spoken for a while, Prakash raised the subject of their going to Manikgunj, again. 'And Manda has not recuperated fully. I am a little hesitant to accompany her on the journey all by myself. It would be wonderful if you came along with us.'

Surama's baffled mind suddenly found something to hold on to and steady itself. Of course, how could she send Manda only with Prakash, considering the state of her health? Surama did not realize that she had been subconsciously looking for an excuse to bargain with her proud ego. So far, her sense of self, though much reduced in its might, had been staring in red-eyed anger at the moves she was contemplating. The pretext she had suddenly found for visiting Manikgunj became a way to appease her ego.

She asked eagerly, 'Are you not comfortable enough to take her there all by yourself?'

'No,' said Prakash.

'What can be done, then?'

'You must come with us.'

'If there is no other way out, I am ready to accompany you. But, Prakash, give me your word that...'

'That what?'

'You would bring me back.'

Prakash had never seen Surama so nervous. It did not surprise him, though. He had an inkling of how his relative was struggling with conflicting emotions. So, he smiled affectionately and said, 'You are going to your own place, Surama. Why be so uneasy?'

'My place? No Prakash. I don't have a place anywhere in this world.'

'You are wrong. Be sure you are the Lakshmi of *this* house. Of course, I will bring you back. What would we do without you?'

'Manda is the Lakshmi of this house, now. Keep her happy for the well-being of this family.'

Prakash laughed. 'Let me tell you something. Don't get angry. You are incapable of feeling at home even in places which are especially meant for you. That makes you so unsettled in your mind. That's why Goddess Lakshmi prefers to keep away from you.'

'Whatever that means. Now, tell me when are we going to Manikgunj?'

'Tomorrow. Start packing.'

'Tomorrow itself? Why not defer it for a few days?' Surama was still scared and felt a trembling within. Naturally, she wanted to postpone the visit. Prakash, however, did not agree.

When Manda expressed how glad she was that they would soon be going to Manikgunj, Surama, holding the younger girl's hand, begged her, 'But, bring me back with you, Manda, when you return.' Surama had no confidence in her own resolve.

Manda supposed that her Ma was wary of Charu's desire

to hold her back. So, she said, 'I will make them understand, Ma, that my claim on you is more than theirs—that I need you, badly, to be with me here.'

Chapter 14

Four years! Four long years had passed by, but everything looked the same to Surama. The tall *jhao* trees, as if exhaling heavily, shook noisily in the breeze. The steeple of a temple, with a *chakra*[33] on it, appeared at a distance. The white walls of the zamindar's palatial residence, the marble staircase leading up to the main hall, the wide green lawn adorned with patches of flowering plants and shrubs, and the path of reddish pebbles running through the lawn, were all just as she had left them.

Soon, the resplendent, white-pillared main hall of the house was directly in front of her.

The car stopped at the gate—exactly at the spot where, four years ago, Surama had entered another limousine after parting from Amar.

Prakash got down from the vehicle immediately, but Surama stayed back in the car to steady herself. Her legs were shaking. After a while, making sure nobody was watching, she came out. The palanquin,[34] in which Manda

---

[33] A wheel or a discus. It is often associated with Lord Vishnu as his weapon.
[34] It seems, in Nirupama Devi's time, a palanquin, rather than a car, was used when extra comfort for the traveller was desired. In this chapter, we come to know that travelling from Kaligunj to Manikgunj involved a short train journey followed by an hour's drive in a car at slow speed (to make the car and the palanquin arrive at the destination almost at the same time).

had travelled from the railway station, had also arrived by then. Manda was just about to disembark by herself when Surama hurriedly came to her aid. With great care, Surama helped Manda to step onto the ground and continued to support her. While Surama was thus occupied, someone from behind grabbed her hand and in a surprised voice exclaimed, 'Is that Didi?'

Surama did not answer or look back. Slowly, her hand was released.

Manda tried to bend down and touch Charu's feet—for, of course, the person who had come to welcome her was Charu. Though Charu tried to dissuade the infirm girl from bending down, Manda, smilingly, offered her pronam. 'How thin you have become!' exclaimed Charu.

Surama and Manda slowly moved into the house. Surama was still supporting the teenager. Charu followed them, amazed at her didi's rude behaviour. The old maidservants of the house offered Surama their namaskar. They, however, did not dare to speak on seeing their mistress so grave. They only spoke to one another in whispers.

The trio entered a bedroom, where Manda was made to sit on the bed. 'Lie down, Manda,' Surama said softly.

'I don't need to, Ma. I feel fine. Aunty, where are Atul and Khuki?'

'Probably in the garden,' replied Charu, mechanically. Surama's coldness had crushed her spirit.

A maid entered the room to announce that the gentlemen of the house were coming to meet them. Surama quickly slipped into an adjoining room. She suddenly felt ashamed that she had come to meet Amar. Her head throbbed. Why did she undertake this venture? Even an hour earlier, when they had reached the railway station, she could have changed her plans. Now, there was no way out. She wished with all her heart to be elsewhere. She would have given her whole life to be back in Kaligunj. Amar must have heard by now or would soon hear that she had come. What would be his reaction? She had once been a proud and arrogant member of his household. Then, breaking all bonds, spurning the love and esteem she was being given there, she had gone to live elsewhere. And today? She had come uninvited to beg for the treasures she had scornfully left behind. What a shame! How could she fall so low? Would she ever be able to recover her lost dignity?

Atul, Amar and Prakash entered the bedroom. Charu and Manda immediately covered their heads. Amar came and sat in a corner of Manda's bed. Prakash remained at a distance and started a pleasant chit-chat with Atul.

'Dear Manda, I came to know about your illness only after our return from Rajputana. How emaciated you look! Rajputana is well known for its healthy climate. When you are a little stronger, Manda, join us for a holiday there. You will recover faster.'

'Thank you, Uncle,' said Manda. She climbed down the bed and paid her respects to him by touching his feet.

After blessing her, Amar asked, 'Have you met Atul? There he is. Atul, come here.'

Atul, a trim eight-your-old, came and stood near the bed. 'How tall you have become, Atul!' she said. 'Do you remember me?'

'Yes, I do. You are my younger didi.'

Amar looked at Charu and said, 'Let Manda have some refreshments.' Looking at Prakash, he said, 'Come, Prakash, let us go out and let the ladies relax. Come, Atul, let us go.'

Charu asked, 'Can Atul be with us for a while?'

'Why not? Atul, your mother wants you to be with them.'

Amar left the room. Surama was overhearing the conversation from the adjoining room. Prakash, she realized, had not informed Amar that she would also be coming from Kaligunj.

She heard footsteps. Somebody wearing footwear was entering the room. Was that Amar?[35] Extremely nervous, she prayed that the ground would open up and swallow her.

A gentle voice called, 'Ma!' Instantly, Surama felt calmer. She turned swiftly to face her caller. It was Atul, her very own Atul! Though his voice had got a little thicker with time, its tone had not changed. His address, 'Ma', sounded as full of affection as it always did.

Atul came closer and held Surama's aanchal. 'Why are you standing here all alone, Ma? Were you hiding from me?'

Surama stretched her arms and wrapped them around him. Atul's voice and touch, on that occasion, warmed her heart more than they had ever done before. And he said, 'You know, Ma, we have bought a pair of beautiful pigeons and a young antelope. Silly Khuki is scared to go near the antelope, though she thinks it belongs to her. She says, "Amal, amal."[36] Why are you hiding here, Ma? Come and see our animals.'

Moved by Atul's comforting words, Surama smiled with

---

[35] The narrative, here, suggests that it was generally men, and not women, who wore sandals at home in Bengal during Nirupama Devi's time.

[36] As Khuki cannot yet pronounce 'r', she is unable to say 'amar amar', which mean 'mine, mine' in Bengali.

an effort and said, 'I will come. But a little later.'

'If you can manage, Ma, come to visit them in the evening. That is the time when I feed them. Look,' Atul continued, 'look at silly Khuki. Is she trying to kill that poor kitten?'

Surama turned and found that a baby girl of about three years of age, as charming as a bud of lily, was watching the two of them in rapt attention. A tiny kitten was hanging from her hand where she had gripped it by the back of its neck. The baby let the kitten go when Surama stretched an arm and lifted her up. However, the child kept on staring at Surama's face, intrigued.

'You know, Ma,' said Atul, 'she can't remember a thing. After coming back from Rajputana, she couldn't recognize this house as our real home and wept, "Take me home, take me home..." And you know, Ma, she only likes to be with our mother. She doesn't know anybody else.'

Slighted by the criticism, Khuki tried to defend herself, 'I also know Baba and Motu and Aja.'

That made Atul laugh heartily. 'Ma, can you follow her? She can't pronounce her r's. So, she calls Raja, Aja. Raja is one of the pigeons. The other is called Rani. Motu is Motru, the antelope.'

Mesmerized by the soothing sounds of Atul's delivery, Surama had not noticed that Charu had entered the room. Khuki leaned towards her mother. Atul commented immediately, 'Watch the fun. She has seen her mother. So, no other company will do for her.'

Ignoring Khuki, Charu bent down and touched Surama's feet. 'How are you, Didi?' she said.

'Good,' was Surama's monosyllabic reply as she pretended to be too busy in comforting Khuki, who was pouting at her mother's snub. Then, Surama sat down on the ground with the kids and found something to engage them.

Charu watched the three of them for a while. Then she caught hold of her didi's hand and tried to pull her up. 'Let us go and bathe, Didi, before we have our lunch,' she said.

Surama remembered Manda. 'Manda needs to eat something now...' she said.

'She has eaten,' said Charu. Now let us go and bathe.'

Surama followed Charu in silence. The house staff she met on her way did not express any surprise at her sudden arrival and behaved as if she had always been there. Surama was sure that they did that at Charu's instructions. She felt genuinely grateful to Charu for that.

After lunch, Atul and Khuki kept Surama busy the whole afternoon and a good part of the evening. She was forced to listen to all the details of how their pets—the antelope, the pigeons, the rabbits, the guinea pigs and the white mice—behaved. She took the kids' leave just once to check on Manda and was relieved to find Manda sitting up and happily gossiping with Charu. 'Ma, may I skip my medicine today? I feel so well,' said Manda as soon as Surama was there. Surama did not have the heart to refuse.

Atul was there to take her back. 'Hurry up, Ma. I'm going to feed Motru now. Come and see.'

'Atul, won't you let her be with us for a while?' ventured Charu.

'No, no. No time for her to sit and talk now.' Atul held Surama's hand and pulled her away.

Getting her away from the adults, the kids had saved Surama a lot of discomfort. The innocence of their words, laughter and looks could not but calm her heart.

After dusk, exhausted by the day's excitement and exertion, Khuki fell asleep on the large bed where Manda had fallen asleep, too. Surama was reclining next to Khuki. Atul had gone to his tutor for his lessons.

'Are you sleepy, Didi?' Charu asked.

'Yes,' said Surama, drowsily.

'No wonder. You have travelled today.'

'Are you very angry with me, Didi?'

'Angry? No,' said Surama, sounding drowsy.

'Aren't you angry because I haven't written to you for so long? Remember, after what happened in Varanasi, I had stopped asking for your news, and had stopped writing to you about us.'

Surama did not say anything. So, Charu continued, 'I now know that that was very irresponsible of me. But, for some time, after that incident in Varanasi, I felt terribly hurt and angry. I thought if you were really uninterested in our lives, what was the use of urging you to be one of us?'

Surama wished to say something but could not find the words. Charu moved still closer. 'Didi, please forgive me for taking that liberty.'

'Charu, let us talk of something else.'

'I can't think of anything else. You haven't called my name or spoken nicely to me since you came here...'

'That was not out of anger, Charu.'

'Oh!'

'Let me tell you the truth, then. It is not anger but shame that is making me so uneasy. I have forced myself to come here just to seek your forgiveness.'

'So, you haven't come to see how we were doing?'

'No. What right have I to do that after the way I behaved

with you? But I am sure I still have the right to seek your forgiveness.'

'Don't apologize to me, Didi. You have done me no wrong. If you think you have mistreated somebody else, tell him that you are sorry, if you can.'

'Yes, I will do that,' blurted Surama, her words sounding like those of a puppet speaking its part.

That evening, Amar, stretched on his bed, was glancing through the newspaper.

'Hello! What are you busy with?' asked Charu.

'Reading, as you can see. Where were you the whole day? Couldn't see a trace of you in this part of the house. How has Manda been? Prakash was worried that she might have a fever again after the strain of the journey.'

'Touch wood, that did not happen. She is sleeping peacefully now. I have come to tell you something really special.'

'What?'

'We have an important guest at home.'

'Who?'

'Someone you know very well. Can you guess who it is?'

Thinking over it for a few seconds, Amar asked, 'A man or a woman?'

'A woman.'

'A woman in need of something?'

'That's right.'

'What does she need?'

'She'd ask for it herself.'

'Stop talking in riddles. Who is she?'

'She is Atul's ma.'

Startled, Amar looked at Charu incredulously.

'Shall I call her in?' asked Charu.

'No. Wait. Tell me clearly. Who is this person you are speaking of?'

'It's Didi. Didi has come.'

'I don't believe it. I was not told about it till now. I am sure Atul would have told me if...'

'I had asked Atul to keep it a secret as I wanted to give you the news first.'

'Now that you have done that, you may leave.'

'Leave and go where?'

'To attend to your honourable guest.'

'She hasn't come here to have a treat. She has come to see Atul and to ask for your forgiveness.'

'There you start with your riddles again! Forgiveness from whom? Forgiveness for what?'

'If somebody had offended somebody...'

'That "somebody" must be you, Charu. And remember that she is your guest today. If you can, excuse her faults.'

'It is not about me, my good husband. An older sister can never wrong her younger sister. It's because *you* are displeased with her that...'

'Enough of that nonsense. I need some peace of mind now. Let me go and see what Prakash is doing.'

Charu stood in front of him saying, 'I won't let you go until you have heard everything.'

'Charu, you are acting silly today. Tell me without any preamble what you want to say.'

'Didi has come. She has come to say sorry to you. Stop being angry with her.'

'Who is she to displease me or make me angry? And I don't care who needs my forgiveness for whichever fault of theirs. Let me go and chat with Prakash.'

Amar left in a huff. Charu kept standing in the middle of the room for a long time. She was in deep thought.

'Where have you been, Charu?' asked Surama when she came to her. 'Atul was looking for you after completing his studies.'

'Just over there,' said Charu, dryly.

'The gentlemen of the house are having their meal. Won't you attend to them?'

'I will. I am going there now. Has Atul eaten?'

'Yes. I took him to the dining hall and gave him his dinner.'

Chapter 15

Seven or eight days passed. Prakash said, 'Dear Manda. I have been away from Kaligunj for over a week and need to go back now. I hope you don't mind staying back here, as your uncle and aunt do not want to leave you so soon.'

Not happy with the proposal, Manda said, 'It would be better if I could go back with you. Can you be here for a few more days and then take me back with you?'

'But our elders here want you to stay with them longer than that.'

'I'll make them understand. I am sure they won't mind if we all return after a few days.'

Manda had just completed her sentence when Surama entered the room. She said, 'Prakash, I think it is about time we returned to Kaligunj. When are you planning to leave?'

Prakash looked at Surama and paused.

'Why are you staring at me?' asked Surama. 'Tell me, when are we going back?'

'Manda suggests we can go back together if I can manage to be away from Kaligunj for a few more days.'

'Will your work permit that?'

'I think a few more days won't make a difference.'

'But then, Manda, too, would be going away soon. Charu is bound to be disappointed.'

'Ma, I know you can reason with her and tell her why I need to go back early,' said Manda.

'I will try.'

Two more days passed. Charu was a little upset that Manda would leave them so soon, but she did not attempt to dissuade her. 'Didi, she is married and has other responsibilities. Let her be well and happy wherever she is,' she said, to Surama's relief.

Nobody requested Surama herself to stay back.

Another two days passed in finalizing the date and time of their departure. Then, only one day remained before their scheduled departure.

Amar had taken care not to see Surama while she stayed in the house. So, Surama decided to go ahead and discharge what she perceived as one of her solemn duties. She had been able to crush much of her arrogance. Now, she had to summon the courage to fully surrender her ego, which would be the final act. Once she accomplished this, her conscience would be clear, leaving no debt unpaid. She would have to say 'yes' to someone, the very person to whom she had once given a negative answer, standing at the exact spot where it was done. She would have to say, 'The curse is in my fate—it is what being a woman has brought me. It is what God has willed for me. My Lord, you have won. Accept the ashes of my vanquished pride. Mark my forehead with it and bless me as I bow to thee. End my heart's torture. Be satisfied. Let there be no need for me to come here again. I am begging you to release me.'

It was their day of departure. Surama received two letters that morning. The one from her father said:

Child, how happy I am! That such a day would come during my lifetime was beyond my imagination. Wish you both a happy, healthy and long life together. I will probably be there soon to wish you in person. Uma will come with me.

I am ending this note for today.

Your father.

Surama realized with irritation that Prakash was to blame for giving Radhakishore the wrong impression. The zamindar had come to believe that his daughter was in her marital home to live there for good. She resolved to correct his misconception without delay.

The second letter was from Uma:

Dear Ma,

Prakash Dada wrote to us, saying that you are in your marital home. It made me very happy. But more than that, it made me angry with you because you have not taken me there along with you. But don't worry, I will soon land up there uninvited. It is my home too as my Ma lives there. In that Kailash, I will adore my Ma with Bholanath next to her.[37]

Ma, I have always seen you in plain clothes. Now, I am eager to see you as the resplendent consort of Bholanath. There, you have Manda and Prakash Dada, along with your other loved ones. Only I am absent. Don't you miss me? I am sure you do.

---

[37] Bholanath is another name for Shiva. Kailash is Shiva's mythical abode where he lives with his consort, Parvati.

How is Atul? Hope he has not forgotten me. Convey my pronam to Aunty. Tell her that I will be there soon. My pronam to you and my baba. Pronam to Prakash Dada and love to Manda. Hope she remembers me.

I will end now.

Your loving daughter,

Uma

Surama tried to laugh at Uma's weird expressions but instead tears rolled down her cheeks. She still wanted to lead the life of a single woman, going against even her own innermost impulses. A hidden struggle in her heart and mind was pulling her apart. But who cared? The world at large was already convinced of her final defeat. Born as a woman, she was expected to act like one. How wretched was the paradigm of her birth!

The day was almost over. The journey was scheduled for later in the evening. Atul looked sad when Surama took him in her arms and put him down again. When she came to Charu, the latter looked down and pretended to concentrate on her housework. Surama was edgy the whole day, with cold hands and feet and a dry mouth. She avoided meeting people to hide her nervousness.

After sunset, lamps were lit in the rooms. Charu approached Surama and called, 'Didi!'

'What?'

'Don't know what to say.'

'Then, don't say anything.'

'But is it the last time of our being together?'

'Yes, it is.'

'Then, go and see him.'

'Yes, I will. Where is he now?'

'In his room. He came in a while ago. Said he had some work at home.'

Surama stood up, ready to go.

'Didi, hurry up. Don't delay it any longer.'

'Then, don't call me 'Didi' so affectionately. Call me something else.'

'Why?'

'Because I am going there today as a real rival-wife—as your competitor.'

'Please do that. Please give me the pleasure of having you that way. Why don't you claim what is rightfully yours? Let me serve you both as a junior.'

Surama sounded grave as she said, 'That's what I am doing. I am going to meet him today not as your facilitator but as his principal wife.'

Charu touched Surama's feet quickly and said endearingly, 'And let that not be only for this meeting. Let that be for a lifetime...'

Surama left the room and went along the long veranda without stopping and stood in front of another room, the chamber in which, more than a decade ago, as a young bride, she had met her husband. She was a vain and arrogant teenager then, basking in her own self-importance. How different as a person she was now!

Amar, his back towards the door, was doing paperwork under a lamp. Sensing somebody breathing heavily behind him, he got up from his chair and turned. Stunned by what he saw, he moved back with a jerk—a lighted matchstick had fallen on a heap of ammunition!

The vision before him did not move. Amar's instincts told him to run away, but he forced himself to stay where he was. In front of him stood the yogini he had seen worshipping Vishwanath in Varanasi. She looked more resplendent, even though she was neither elegantly attired nor had her palms joined together.

Surama came forward, kneeled, and was about to touch Amar's feet with her brow when he quickly moved back.

'Don't you wish to accept my pronam?' asked Surama.

'No.'

'Why?'

'I have my reasons.'

'I am your visitor. Should we not greet each other?'

'I need to go out now. If you have come to me on some business, tell me directly what it is. Otherwise...'

'First of all, I came just to meet you...'

'Now that we have met, can I leave?'

'Of course.'

Amar, however, did not leave the room at once. It looked like he, too, wanted to say something but was trying to restrain himself. After a few seconds, as Surama just stood there without speaking, he said, 'If you have come to me just to say goodbye, let me tell you that it was not required.'

Surama still did not speak. Amar continued, 'Charu says you wanted to be forgiven. Is that true?'

'Yes.'

'Forgiven for what? Because you had suddenly left Varanasi? Charu is silly enough to be hurt by that. As for myself, who am I to be offended by your behaviour? Am I not a "nobody" to you?'

The words pinched Surama. She felt a chill inside

her. She was timid and nervous. One day, four years ago, she had said something so forcefully that it had left Amar dumbfounded. Right now, she had a different message for him. Could she deliver it with the same conviction?

Amar went on, 'Do you suppose I was distressed in any way by your mistreatment of us? I was not. Don't you remember what you said to me the last time we met? You had ended our relationship at that instant. There was no need, therefore, for you to come to me today for leave-taking. We took leave of each other a long time ago.'

Surama was looking down at the floor. Amar came closer to her. As Surama was still silent, he said, 'Not much time left for you to start your journey.'

Surama looked at the door and turned to move but Amar approached swiftly and stood before her. He said, 'Didn't you say you had come to me for some business, too?'

Surama nodded.

'But you are leaving.'

Surama rebuked herself. Why was she still holding back her confession? Why was she still unable to rise above her ego? Shame on her! She straightened herself and cleared her voice. And she said, 'You had asked me a question on the day I left you. I have come here today with my answer.'

'You had given me an answer right away...' said Amar.

'I did not speak the truth that time,' said Surama. 'I am a woman. Mother Nature has not given me the right to hate. A woman can't be arrogant, vain, or haughty. She has...'

'She has what, Surama? She has only the right to take revenge?'

'No. She has the right only to love unconditionally. She has the right to devote herself to her superiors. And she has the right to...'

Surama had moved a little towards the door. Amar came closer and held her hand. He said, 'And she has the right to what? Complete your sentence before you go.'

Surama sat down where she was and wrapped her hands around Amar's ankles. With tears rolling down her cheeks, she said, 'And the right to a peaceful place like this. Here is my home. Do not make me an exile again.'

Acknowledgements

My tribute to Nirupama Devi's memory and my obligations to my publishers. I owe a lot to Mr Dibakar Ghosh for his guidance and to Ms Veeksha Vagmita for her skilful editing.

A big 'Thank You' to Shyamali Sarkar for giving me the Bengali Complete Works of Nirupama Devi just when I was desperately looking for a good copy of *Didi*. That volume enabled me to begin my project of translation.

I am indebted to my sister-in-law Anita Shome for lending me a rare book of essays written soon after Sarat Chandra's demise. The collection includes an essay by Nirupama Devi herself where she provides us with a glimpse of her relationship with Sarat Chandra. It helped me to get a realistic view of that aspect of Nirupama's life.

I extend my sincere thanks to Suva Sarkar, my cousin sister, for sharing with me an article on Nirupama Devi by Sudeshna Basu.

I am deeply grateful to Sunanda Rudra, my cousin sister, for giving me the Bengali meanings of the Sanskrit words used in *Didi*.

Affection and praise for my husband Samir Kumar Shome for being there for me always. Even though he passed away with a weak heart and Covid on 18 July 2022, I feel his presence every moment of my life. How thrilled he would have been to hold *Didi*, published by Rupa, in his hands!

Gentle thoughts for our wonderful children, Siddhartha and Alaknanda, and our son-in-law, Soumitra. Love to Amalina and Nivedita—our gorgeous granddaughters.

I miss my only sibling, Uday Dutta (1949–2021). He was not only a brother to me but also a friend, philosopher and guide who took keen interest in my work. Though younger to me by four years, he never called me *Didi*.